She laid a hand on his shoulder, reconsidered a moment, then sent her other hand southward

Hardening instantly, Tyler sucked in a breath.

"I've been thinking about fantasies," Andrea said softly, stroking him.

"Yeah?" His voice was little more than a whisper.

"Remember how we broke several traffic laws in the squad car last night?"

His erection pulsed. "Vividly."

"Well, there's another one where I get naked in the sheriff's office."

"We're not in the sheriff's office."

She grabbed the hem of her sundress and lifted it over her head. "Then we'll have to make do with what we've got."

Blaze

Dear Reader,

Back to Palmer's Island!

If you haven't stuck your toes in the sand or been introduced to the fun and eccentric islanders yet, then welcome. My fictional island is a combination of two real places in South Carolina—Isle of Palms and Sullivan's Island. In addition to allowing me to write off my trips there (*research*, you know), they've inspired a world that I hope you'll want to come to again and again.

The Atlantic breezes tend to inspire lots of romance—of course—and this time you'll meet Tyler Landry and Andrea Hastings, who've both moved back to the home where they were raised and find themselves seeing each other in a whole new light.

Unfortunately, while the sheriff's out of town and Deputy Landry is hoping to be elected to succeed the revered lawman, there's a "serial silver stealer" on the loose. The famous task force (which includes a nun, two church ladies and a librarian) is reassembled in the hopes of ending the crime spree and getting the peaceful island back to normal.

Happy Valentine's Day!

Wendy Etherington

Wendy Etherington

TEMPT ME AGAIN

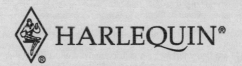

TORONTO • NEW YORK • LONDON
AMSTERDAM • PARIS • SYDNEY • HAMBURG
STOCKHOLM • ATHENS • TOKYO • MILAN • MADRID
PRAGUE • WARSAW • BUDAPEST • AUCKLAND

Recycling programs
for this product may
not exist in your area.

ISBN-13: 978-0-373-79528-4

TEMPT ME AGAIN

Copyright © 2010 by Etherington, Inc.

This edition published by arrangement with Harlequin Books S.A.

® and TM are trademarks of the publisher. Trademarks indicated with ® are registered in the United States Patent and Trademark Office, the Canadian Trade Marks Office and in other countries.

www.eHarlequin.com

Printed in U.S.A.

ABOUT THE AUTHOR

Wendy Etherington was born and raised in the deep South—and she has the fried chicken recipes and NASCAR ticket stubs to prove it. The author of nearly twenty books, she writes full-time from her home in South Carolina, where she lives with her husband and two daughters.

Books by Wendy Etherington

HARLEQUIN BLAZE
263—JUST ONE TASTE...
310—A BREATH AWAY
385—WHAT HAPPENED IN VEGAS...
446—AFTER DARK

HARLEQUIN NASCAR
HOT PURSUIT
FULL THROTTLE
NO HOLDING BACK, with Liz Allison
RISKING HER HEART, with Liz Allison

Don't miss any of our special offers. Write to us at the following address for information on our newest releases.

Harlequin Reader Service
U.S.: 3010 Walden Ave., P.O. Box 1325, Buffalo, NY 14269
Canadian: P.O. Box 609, Fort Erie, Ont. L2A 5X3

To my editor, Kathryn Lye, for her insight,
valiant revisions and never-ending patience.
Thanks a bunch!

1

"I THINK YOU OUGHT to seduce him."

Andrea Hastings turned her surprised gaze toward her friend, who was currently binding her into the breath-stealing corset necessary to give authenticity to her early-nineteenth-century costume ball gown. "How the devil am I supposed to do that?"

Sloan Caldwell Kendrick simply—and wickedly—raised her eyebrows.

Andrea scoffed and faced the full-length antique oval mirror again. "I know how in the technical sense…"

"But not so much in the practical. You're too smart for your own good. I've got a book—"

Andrea waved her away. Being Palmer's Island's librarian, Sloan always had a book. "Get real. I'm not going to seduce Tyler Landry with printed instructions."

Sloan smiled wide. "There are illustrations, too."

Closing her eyes, Andrea felt her face heat. Despite her confident exterior, she still had a hard time with emotional vulnerability, and she considered sex to be the ultimate moment of exposure.

Especially with Tyler.

Well, she *assumed* with Tyler.

She'd tutored him in high school math and had fallen

like a brick for his easy smile and bright blue eyes. His ability to excel in everything except algebra had earned him a scholarship to the Naval Academy, and, at the beach party the night before he was due to leave, she'd offered herself to him.

To, hopefully, find the G-spot, not the x- and y-axis.

He'd either been too embarrassed or too noble to accept. She'd never found out which, since she'd run away like a silly little girl, which she'd certainly been.

In the years since, she'd tried to think like her high school buddy Sloan—confident and willing to take a chance. Professionally, she'd succeeded. In her personal life…not so much.

She'd had lovers; she'd moved on. But she still burned a ridiculous, unrealistic candle—okay, flaming torch—for Tyler. It was an embarrassment, something a woman who'd traveled the world, who worked for a global insurance company, who knew art, history and finances, who freakin' specialized in spotting forgeries, should be able to shrug off without a backward glance.

Sloan jerked the corset strings again, then tied them.

Andrea winced. "Authenticity, my ass."

"Actually, the authenticity is necessary for your *waist*." Sloan turned away to snag the elaborate lace-and-silk gown off the bed. "And aren't you always telling me the proof is in the details?"

It's pretty crappy to have your own words thrown back at you on a regular basis.

That's what recently moving back to her South Carolina island home had gotten her—old friends she couldn't snow with her degrees and put-upon self-assurance. People like Sloan knew she was a nerd—always had been, always would be—but still thought she was pretty great anyway.

"The details in my industry involve lots of chemistry," Andrea pointed out.

"Good. So does seduction."

As Sloan dropped the frothy gown over her head, Andrea focused on the anticipation of the party that was due to start in less than an hour. Her friend and her husband, Aidan—who could challenge even Tyler for the Hot and Beautiful Man of Palmer's Island prize—had organized a fund-raiser with an 1812 theme to support the efforts of the island's historical society, of which Sloan was a dedicated member.

Together, Sloan and Aidan had restored an elegant, nineteenth-century home to its former glory so that now Batherton Mansion was once again a prize of island preservation.

Staring in the mirror as Sloan snapped, hooked and bound her into her costume, Andrea watched herself be transformed from the practical insurance appraiser into an elegant lady of the past.

The pale blue silk and white lace trimmed gown hugged her curves, which she certainly had more of after the torturous corset did its thing, boosting her bust to new heights. And either her self-consciousness or the lack of oxygen to her brain had caused a nice flush to her cheeks. Her light green eyes were highlighted from Sloan's makeup job and bright with promise. Her golden-blond hair, lifted in ringlet curls, exposed her neck and the throbbing pulse just below her jaw.

Andrea braced her palm against her stomach. "It's quite a switch."

Laying her hands on Andrea's shoulders, Sloan met her gaze in the mirror. "You look amazing."

She wasn't sure it was her—though with her devotion to history, it somehow *should* be. Certainly the charade wouldn't last, but it would be fun to pretend to be the beauty instead of the brains for one night. She lifted her fingers to her face. "Are we sure that's me in there?"

Sloan's eyes narrowed with annoyance. "Of course it is. Aren't you the one who walked me through the Met and the Louvre?"

"That doesn't have anything to do with—"

"Sure it does. You know your art and you show it. You know you're desirable and you show it."

There was logic in there somewhere, but Andrea still somehow felt her words were being turned on her. Like she was on a ledge and being pushed into a bottomless abyss of confusion and uncertainty.

Gee, Andrea, dramatic much?

She hugged her friend as much as the wide-skirted dresses would allow. When they leaned back, the anxiety that had fluttered almost constantly in her stomach since her old crush moved back to the island last month intruded again. She met her friend's gaze. "But am I ready to face Tyler Landry?"

Sloan braced her hands on her hips. "Hell, yes."

Eyeing Sloan in her plum-colored-satin and black-lace dress, her voluptuous body seemingly made for seduction, Andrea laughed. "*You* certainly are."

"I'll stick with my husband, thanks." She paused, angling her head. "Come to think of it, that's whose advice you need."

"What am I? A community project? Hey, let's finally give the geek girl her dream night with her forbidden crush."

Sloan steered her from the bedroom suite into the hall. "You're not a geek, and he might have been somewhat out of reach before, but not forbidden. Now, he's certainly neither."

"Maybe not in the personal sense." Though Andrea still couldn't imagine looking Tyler in the eye and inviting him into her bed. That was disturbing. Where had her nerve gone? Why did she have to let this one man get to her so thoroughly? Maybe he'd take one glance at her and invite her into *his* bed.

Hey, if she was going to fantasize, she might as well give it her all.

"He's running for sheriff," she said to Sloan. "He needs to win votes. Even your dad's endorsement might not save him if he does something scandalous. You know how people talk on the island."

"You're planning on taking out an ad?" Those brazen eyebrows winged up again *"I finally screwed the delicious Tyler Landry! Check my blog for pictures!"*

"Oh, sure. I'll be sure to send copies to my boss, too."

"Actually," Sloan continued as if Andrea hadn't spoken, "regardless of gossip, naked pictures of him would probably assure victory."

Since Andrea had been avoiding him in the flesh, she only had campaign posters and her teenage memories to fall back on. "He still, you know…looks that good, does he?"

Sloan's bright blue eyes twinkled. "Better."

"I didn't need to know that." Andrea stopped in the hall, on the breezeway overlooking the dramatic two story foyer. "My life is complicated enough. Looking after Finn is a challenge."

"Your brother is twenty, not twelve."

"And I have lots of responsibility at work. The stress—"

"You're working on a consulting basis. You've only taken on three cases since you've been home."

"But when I take them, they're stressful. And I have that big assignment in London next month."

"Uh-huh." Sloan urged Andrea forward again. "Whatever. This doesn't have to be complicated. You don't have to marry the man. It's one night."

"Is that what you told yourself when you met Aidan?"

"Naturally."

"Somehow, that's not encouraging."

"Since when are you opposed to marrying the man of your dreams?"

"When he comes along, I won't be."

"Why can't Tyler be him?"

"Sure. Right."

"Why not?" Sloan insisted.

Andrea stared at her. "He's him, and I'm me."

"Sure," Sloan said, her sarcasm clear. "How obvious."

"He's Tyler Landry. War hero. Sports hero. Hometown hero. He's spent the last decade in the Commune For Those Who Are Worshipped As Heroes. He's a *hero*."

"Oh, so he's too good for you."

Suppressing a wince, Andrea placed a hand on the staircase railing as she started down. "It's not about good and bad."

"So it's a level of degrees thing, then. He's up here—" Sloan held her hand high above her head "—and you're not fit to lick his boots."

"Ah…"

"Stupid, right? Stupid is the word you're searching for. Probably." She paused, as if considering. "Or maybe idiotic is better."

Scowling as they reached the foyer, Andrea turned and headed toward the kitchen—only to be nearly mowed down by her brother, running down the hall toward the front door.

"I'm late," he said briefly as he grabbed her shoulders and kissed her cheek.

"And why's that?" she returned, pleased to note he was freshly shaven and his usually spiky blond hair was tamed in a conservative style.

"The Sisters made me rewash the floors in the rec room."

Finn was a convicted felon, but, thankfully, Sister Mary Katherine's latest project. As a result, he worked for the church and had an apartment of his own on the grounds. He was rebuilding his life one brick at a time, and Andrea was proud of his dedication to leaving his old life behind.

"You look nice, Andy, but I gotta go," Finn said, scooting off. "Thanks, Mrs. Kendrick," he called over his shoulder.

Tonight Finn had been hired by her friend to valet park cars during the party. Funny, since he'd gone to prison for boosting one.

Moving toward the kitchen and endeavoring to set aside any worries over her brother, Andrea's thoughts immediately went back to Tyler.

Sloan had a pretty undeniable point about her insecurities involving him. She wasn't a kid anymore, but a grown woman. Why should she be worried about—

She stopped as she noticed the man standing in the kitchen, directing the catering staff, who were rushing about with platters and glasses or stirring luscious-smelling dishes on the stove.

Stunning and darkly gorgeous in period formal wear,

Aidan Kendrick could make any woman at any time forget how to speak, but with the added effect of his bright and lustful smile—aimed at his wife—he was positively drool worthy.

"Does he have a brother?" Andrea whispered to Sloan as Aidan approached them.

"Sorry, no."

"Ladies," Aidan said, then brushed his lips across Andrea's cheek. He slid his arm possessively around Sloan's waist and kissed her as well.

With considerably more and lingering heat.

"It's a good thing I have the new sheriff attending the party," he said, studying them both when he leaned back. "We'll need crowd control to keep the men at bay."

"Tyler hasn't won yet," Sloan said.

"But he will," Andrea assured her.

At her confident tone, Aidan raised his eyebrows. "A fan of Lieutenant Landry?"

How did she clarify? She'd known Aidan only a few months, and explaining she had the hots for a hot guy to an equally hot guy was somehow embarrassing. "He's…"

"The object of her undying worship and lust," Sloan answered, her lips cuving slyly.

"Used to be," Andrea returned, glaring at Sloan. "A long time ago."

Sloan's smile widened. "Right. She's moved on to action these days. Get some of her pride back after the first failed seduction. She's going to succeed this time. I suggested the blue suite."

Andrea clenched her teeth. "Shut up immediately."

Aidan captured Andrea's hand and squeezed. "Self-assured women are irresistible."

Sloan elbowed her husband in the stomach. "Are they really?"

"Certainly." His silver eyes gleamed. "You are their queen, after all."

Seeing the answering desire in her friend's eyes, Andrea started to back up. They were newlyweds, after all. "I'll just…disappear."

"No, don't." Sloan moved away from her husband. "Come check out the decorations with me." She met Aidan's gaze. "If you keep looking at me like that, we'll be late greeting the guests."

"And why would that be a problem?" he asked reasonably. Though he didn't pull her back, his eyes clearly reflected his intention to resume this moment. Later.

With effort, Andrea suppressed the urge to sigh lustfully. Sister Mary Katherine—the spiritual leader of the island—would distinctly not approve. And, of course, Andrea herself knew it was wrong to covet her friend's husband, even in a conceptual, non-skanky way.

"I'll have one of the waitstaff send out champagne for you to enjoy on your tour," he added.

Andrea cast a glance over her shoulder.

Maybe just a mini sigh.

As she left the kitchen with Sloan, her friend whispered, "How can you see that and not be inspired for seduction?"

"I'm definitely hot and bothered. But it could just be the costume cutting off my air supply."

A few minutes later, a tuxedoed waiter approached with a tray, expertly balancing two glasses filled with fizzing champagne. After giving their thanks, Andrea and Sloan headed into the dining room, where, while they'd been getting dressed, the decorator had transformed the period chandelier and formal table with flowers, greenery and candles. Varying shades of green and blue melded together with the golden lights, which wound up somehow being both simple and elaborate. Stuffed peacocks, both large and small, and their feathers accentuated the decor.

One sideboard was lined with chafing dishes, ready to accept the contents of the dishes the caterer and her staff were rushing to finish in the kitchen. Another held sparkling white-and-gold china, crystal and silverware.

"Wow," they said together.

In an impressed haze, they wandered through the foyer and front parlor, which had been given the same treatment. The windows and side door leading to the garden had been left open to catch a cool breeze. While most points north were shivering in mid-October, the island had been enjoying wonderfully balmy days and nights.

As she sipped champagne, the atmosphere, the pep talk and her own transformed appearance sent a burst of excitement through Andrea's veins. Like viewing a priceless work of art for the first time, she felt capable of anything.

And suddenly the idea of seducing Tyler seemed possible.

She'd tried it once without success. Was she crazy to attempt it again? Or did she *have* to try once more, just as Sloan had suggested, to get her pride back, to honor the memory of a nervous girl who longed for someone she'd always known she could never have?

With the memory, though, came resentment. How could she burn a torch and hold on to the anger of her rejection at the same time? Could seduction bring that decade-long dichotomy to a close?

"Oh, Andrea, I nearly forgot." Sloan crossed to a table

set up beside the front door, picked up something black and turquoise, then dangled it on her finger by the elastic strap.

A mask.

With a devious smile on her face, Sloan walked toward her. "Nobody says you have to tell Tyler who, exactly, his seductress is."

Was her buddy brilliant or what?

Tonight, she didn't have to worry about her ex-con brother. She didn't have to face her fellow islanders; she could hide from anyone who'd known her as quiet and plain. She could be exotic and mysterious, alluring and confident— everything she'd always dreamed she could be with Tyler.

Her gaze met and held Sloan's. "You're a genius."

"I know," she said as she slipped the mask over Andrea's face.

TYLER LANDRY ACCEPTED a glass of champagne from a passing waiter as he struggled to keep his attention on one of his—hopefully—future constituents.

In a few short weeks, he'd officially be their law enforcement leader. To serve and protect. As current sheriff, Buddy Caldwell, had done for more than thirty years. As his own grandfather had done before that.

All he had to do was get elected, which he didn't see a problem accomplishing, since he had Buddy's endorsement, and the only other candidate advocated the use of long-bow leather whips instead of guns as a sidearm.

For Indiana Jones, yes. For Lester Cradock, not exactly.

Not that Tyler planned to use his gun that often anyway. He'd done so plenty of times in his decade as a Marine and in many ways didn't mind leaving that violent and unsteady life behind him.

But was rosebush vandalism going to be the highlight of his term as sheriff?

"I mean, some people just don't understand the nuances of roses, particularly a premier hybrid tea."

"I'm sure that's true, Miss Patsy," he said politely.

"It's all about color and bud tightness."

"Uh-huh."

"I've spliced the palest yellow trimmed with bright pink." Her tone took on the familiar fervor—aka obsession—of a true horticultural guru. "It's certain to win the prize this year."

His grandmother had suffered—or maybe thrived— from the same affliction, so Tyler nodded as expected. "I'm sure."

"You're not simply placating me, are you?" she asked, eyes narrowed.

"No, ma'am." Or not a lot anyway. He smiled widely as a young woman walking by sent him a flirty smile and wondered how quickly he could follow her. "I'm riveted to your story."

"If you want to know what's happening on this island, and if you want to eat right while you're on it, you're going to need mine and Betsy's help."

"Yes, ma'am, I'm definitely aware of that."

Patsy Smith and Betsy Johnson were known as the Casserole Twins. And though they were of similar age, they weren't twins or even related, but they did make the best comfort casseroles in the state.

Through every birth, death, graduation, promotion, job loss, tragedy and triumph, they were there, offering food in foil-covered containers and strength in their faith and hope for the future. Their support, as well as their tendency to meddle, had even landed them in the middle of a murder investigation last spring.

"Both my Precious Pink and Sunlit by the Stars roses won first prize in their categories at the state fair last year," Patsy continued.

Part—okay, maybe all—of the perks of having a prize-winning rose was getting to name it. Like submitting a child's name on a birth certificate, this was a long-drawn-out and hotly debated process.

Patsy nibbled a cracker, seeming calm, but not. "The roses are at the end of their blooming cycles and need to be left alone until I cut them back on President's Day."

Tyler paused with his glass of champagne nearly to his lips. "That's in February."

Patsy bobbed her gray-streaked head in agreement. "Exactly my point. By these unscrupulous vandals cutting them now, the tender branches are left vulnerable to the winter elements. They need to hibernate."

"Like bears."

"Of course not like—" She stopped, considering. "Well, perhaps. Cutting encourages growth, and the plants are going dormant, gathering strength to bloom in the spring."

"Like bears."

"Sly." She waggled the finger of one hand while balancing her plate of appetizers with the other. "Your grandfather was the same."

He nodded at the compliment. His parents and grandfather still lived on the island, as his family had for four generations, so he was well aware of the sterling reputation he had to live up to. He'd nearly accomplished that. He'd excelled at sports, distinguished himself in combat and was now on the verge of being a vital community leader.

His family's pride should be safe.

And if that included The Case of the Chopped Rosebush or The Mysterious Disappearance of the Palmetto Trees—which the local landscape architect had already bent his ear about yesterday—then that's what he'd handle.

Wasn't normal and mundane activity what his CO had insisted he needed? Wasn't that why he'd taken early retirement?

The years of blood and death, poverty and frustration, secret missions in the dead of night had taken a toll on his ability to do his job. He'd become too hard and callous, taken too many risks with himself and, to his great regret, his team.

And if the residents of Palmer's Island knew any of that, the only position he'd get elected for would involve gutter cleaning.

After a major hurricane.

Coming back home was about remembering and honoring his roots and maybe reliving a bit of the good ole days, when he was a football champion bound for glory defending his country.

Nobody had to know he'd changed. Nobody had to know he wasn't the hero they remembered. Nobody had to know about his fear of living up to his family legacy.

He could be responsible for cultivating the next Precious Star of the…whatever that flashed on the national rose tabloid scene.

A woman wearing a mask and fluttering a fan in front of her face approached him and Patsy. "Quite a party," the woman said. "Have you tried those mini crab cakes? Yum."

"Good evening, Miss Betsy," Tyler said brightly, in an effort to charm her and hopefully get the conversation off hybrid teas.

The pale blue eyes behind the mask narrowed. "How'd you know it was me?"

"Your eyes are pretty distinctive. I remember them scowling at me during Sunday school many times."

"See, Betsy," Patsy said, nudging her friend, "I told you he'd grown into a sharp boy."

Tyler fought a wince at *boy,* but he supposed he'd always be young to his parents' and grandparents' friends. The fact that he'd graduated with honors from both high school and the Naval Academy, fought in a war and led countless other military missions, would apparently always be superseded by his days coloring pictures of disciples at St. Matthews Catholic Church.

"Why aren't you wearing a mask?" Betsy asked.

There was no way he was going to listen to cracks from his buddies about the Lone Ranger all night—though he had no intention of telling that to the ladies. He ran his fingers over his jaw. "And cover up this perfect face?"

"There's a difference between confidence and conceit," Patsy said, tapping her foot and clearly unmoved by his charm. "Your grandfather knew that, too."

He grinned. "And I don't?"

Patsy's gaze raked him from head to toe. "With a little guidance from us."

After sending her friend a nod of agreement, Betsy laid her hand on his arm. "Now, tell us all about your girlfriend. We haven't heard a thing about her."

"Because I don't have one."

And that was definitely the wrong thing to say.

Both women's eyes lit like fireworks. "Really?" they said in a weirdly simultaneous question that made the hairs on the back of his neck stand straight up.

"My niece just graduated from the College of Charleston," Patsy said.

"There's a lovely young lady who's been volunteering at the church." Betsy squeezed his arm. "She moved back to the island to take care of her grandmother. I could set you two up…"

"I can get my own dates," Tyler returned in a rush, feeling a bubble of panic bloom in his chest. "Really." When they scowled, he added, "But thank you. Really."

"He *was* a heartthrob in high school," Patsy recalled.

Betsy frowned. "Clearly his charm is somehow suffering, if he can't get a date now."

Tyler held up his hands. "Uh, ladies? I can get a date." And he remembered, quite desperately, the woman who'd walked by earlier. Why hadn't he run after her when he'd had the chance? "I just don't have a girlfriend."

The two women glanced at each other, then pinned him with twin glares.

"You need one," Patsy said.

"It's certainly time for you to settle down." Betsy nodded.

Tyler shook his head and vowed not to panic. "No, it isn't. I'm happy being single. I'm good at it."

"Yes," Patsy agreed.

"I'm sure you are," Betsy finished.

"But there comes a time…" Patsy said.

"When even infamous bachelors retire into matrimony," Betsy finished again.

Tyler stepped back. "Well, yeah. But I'm not ready—"

"Hi, Tyler."

He nearly fell to his knees at the sight of the attractive brunette who'd stopped next to him. "Hi, uh…Cheryl? Cheryl Elliott?" When she nodded, he pulled her close for a hug. "I haven't seen you in years. Maybe not since high school graduation. You look great. How are you?"

"Fine," she said, her eyes bright with interest. "It's so good to see you. You look better than ever. And how is that possible?"

He shrugged. "Clean living."

Cheryl winked. "Oh, sure."

"Hello, Ms. Elliot," Patsy said.

"Or is it *Mrs.?*" Betsy asked.

"Could the divorce proceedings be over that quickly?" Patsy asked.

"My, how time does fly," Betsy said, looking amazed and fooling nobody.

Cheryl made a quick and embarrassed exit.

Tyler sighed. "You two are ruining my night."

The Casserole Twins each gripped one of his arms. "Don't upset yourself," Patsy said.

Betsy glared at him. "But, remember, if you want to be sheriff, you need us. So be nice."

Tyler now knew how the fly in a spider's web felt. His comfortable bachelorhood hanging in the balance, he prodded, "When have I not been nice? You're the ones running off my chances to—" it would probably be better if he modified that thought before it escaped "—to meet nice girls I could possibly, someday, settle down with and make babies for you to teach in Sunday school."

The two women exchanged skeptical glances.

"We raised four boys and three girls between us," Patsy said.

"Do we really look that dumb?" Betsy asked.

"Definitely not. Still, I—" Tyler stopped as his attention was caught by a woman entering the parlor from the dining

room. She wore a pale blue satin gown and mask of pea-
cock feathers. Even with her face obscured, her sculpted
cheeks and the feminine line of her jaw hinted at her
delicate beauty. Her lips were full and deep red. Her golden
hair was pulled up, exposing the delicate column of her
throat, leaving ringlet curls to barely brush her shoulders,
and the costume cinched her waist and lifted her breasts,
leaving no doubt about the curvy delights that lay beneath.

She was a vision from the past, though the confident
way she moved across the room was completely modern.

The contrast made his mouth go dry.

"Who's that?" he asked, his gaze fixed to the blonde
like a magnet.

Patsy turned her head. "Well, now. I don't really
know. Betsy?"

"No idea." Betsy patted his shoulder. "But we'll certainly find out."

2

"YOU LOOK THIRSTY," a male voice said from behind Andrea.

Turning, she barely avoided jolting at the sight of the gorgeous, blue-eyed man who held out a glass of champagne.

Tyler Landry.

She hadn't recognized his voice. But then that was hardly surprising, after not hearing it for more than a decade. Swallowing, she fought for words, the right tone. There were lines in his face that hadn't been there before. His eyes had a sharper edge that most probably wouldn't notice, but she did, as she'd spent hours studying pictures of him and wondering how she'd feel, how she'd react, if those perfect baby blues had ever focused on her for more than a millisecond.

As they were now.

Oh, boy.

Heart hammering, she fought for something clever to say. He knew her as a nerd and hadn't wanted her. Would he really change his mind now? Underneath it all, she wasn't any different.

She flicked a glance at the glass he held and hoped her voice would hold steady. "How far away were you when you noticed my unquenchable thirst?"

He smiled invitingly, a flash of the bright white teeth

that graced storefronts and utility poles all over the island. "On the other side of the room."

"Noticed me from way over there, did you?"

"Definitely."

Her heart jumped against her ribs, but she kept her tone casual. "Maybe I don't like champagne."

His smile dimmed. "I could get you something else."

And there was the innate *niceness* that had always been part of Tyler. He was popular, beautiful and athletic. He could have been a jerk to everybody, and he still would have been worshipped. But, no, he'd been decent and kind. Even to a nerd with braces who couldn't speak to him without stammering.

She plucked the glass from his hand. "But I do like champagne."

He stepped closer. "It suits you—sparkling and elegant."

"Thanks." Her gaze met his, the seductive blue seeming to peer into her soul. She avoided looking at the lustrous, dark brown hair she'd always longed to trail her fingertips through and never had the courage. But she did notice his shoulders were broader, his body still leanly muscled. Still perfect, after all these years.

Did she even dare to inhale too deeply? He probably smelled perfect. Like heaven. Or maybe sin.

She sipped champagne and fought for something witty to say. Glancing around the room, she caught Sloan's gaze. Her friend gave her an enthusiastic thumbs-up, which helped her focus. *What would Sloan say?*

"Do I know you?" she managed to ask. "You look familiar."

He held out his hand. "Tyler Landry. I'm running for sheriff."

As she touched him, she felt the spark of attraction that hadn't, ridiculously, faded after all this time. "I'm…"

Surely you're not crazy enough to make that mistake.

"Glad to meet you," she finished.

"You have a name, too, don't you?"

"I do."

He cocked his head. "But you're not going to tell me what it is."

"No."

"Why?"

"Why should I?"

"So I can get to know you."

"We don't need names for that."

His eyes flashed with shock, regret, then interest.

Wow, oh, wow, it's working.

"Mystery lady, huh?" He grinned and considered her, slowly, from head to toe. "Have we met before?"

Andrea hesitated before realizing he'd never connect her with his braces-and-thick-glasses former math tutor. "Yes."

Though she had his attention before, now she had his interest. "Recently?" he asked.

"No."

"Did we meet on the island? I haven't visited very often, and I only moved back a month ago, so—"

She laid her hand in the center of his chest. "No more questions. You'll spoil the fun."

"Yeah? How much fun are we talking about?"

She licked her lips. "Lots."

His gaze grew intense. "Well, we definitely wouldn't want to ruin it, then."

"Are you alone?"

"Before I saw you I was."

"Then let me show you the house. Do you know the history surrounding it?"

"Only a bit." He linked their hands. "Show me."

With the warmth of his palm pressed against hers, she led him from the parlor and into the dining room, which was equally crowded with guests who were eating, drinking and chatting as if they had no idea of the significance of her and Tyler Landry touching.

Which, thankfully, they didn't.

"The house was built in 1809 by George Batherton, a successful physician and planter of the day. He had a fear of the water, hence the settling two full blocks from the shore."

"But no hence on why he lived on an island in the first place."

"No. We can only assume that his wife, who was a cousin to the Earl of Something-Or-Other, understood the intimate and financial definition of beachfront property."

Tyler nodded. "A wise and progressive woman." He glanced at the elaborate copper chandelier dangling above the dining room table. "And one with excellent taste."

"That's a reproduction, but it certainly fits the period."

He turned his head to stare at her. "Does it?"

Surprised she'd been lured into showing off her historical expertise, she cleared her throat. "Well, so I hear. Life rolled along nicely for his wife and ten kids until an inconvenient skirmish called The War of 1812. Then later the Civil War—"

"Isn't that the War of Northern Aggression?" he asked, and she assumed his tongue was planted firmly in his cheek.

Of course she wanted it somewhere else entirely…

"Considering where we're standing geographically, I suppose it is," she conceded. "Regardless, and obviously, this house is a survivor, since between all those messy battles there were also various hurricanes and years of disrepair. The house has been restored to its old glory by a former Atlanta businessman, who's taken a hands-on approach to restoration. You should see the stair railing he found—"

"Can I see you in the kitchen for a minute?" Sloan asked suddenly from behind her.

Andrea turned to face her friend. "Ah…sure." But she'd just been getting into the rhythm of her story. And how was she supposed to keep Tyler's interest while she was in the kitchen? "I guess you know Tyler," she added, stalling.

"We went to high school together," Tyler said, then his expression turned speculative. His gaze slid back and forth between the two women. "Friends with Sloan, huh? Did *we* go to high school together?"

Panic bubbled in Andrea's stomach. "I, uh…"

"I bet you're one of Sloan's cheerleader friends," he continued. "There were quite a few blondes."

"She's—" Sloan began.

But Tyler rolled on with, "Lana Miller." He snapped his fingers. "Or Amber Dessler. You could be—"

"I'm taking her now," Sloan said, her frustration clear. "I promise to return her eventually." She grasped Andrea's elbow and steered her down the hall. In the kitchen, she dodged various members of the catering staff, then tugged Andrea into a corner. "He doesn't need a history lesson."

"How do you know I was giving him one?"

Sloan simply raised her eyebrows.

Andrea sighed. "Okay, fine. But at least it's something I know. I get history. I don't get seduction."

"You could start by looking at him with at least as much awe and longing as you do the chandelier."

"Ha, ha. And that's my problem, by the way. I'm too in awe of him. I can't relax."

"Which is exactly why I saved you and brought you in here."

"I'm supposed to seduce him from in here?"

"You're supposed to regroup in here."

Andrea leaned back against the wall. "It hardly matters. You heard him. Cheerleader. Yeah, right. He doesn't remember me at all."

Sloan examined her manicure. "My event planner's a little busy at the moment, but I bet you could book him later."

"Book him for what?"

"Your pity party."

"He thinks I'm Lana or Amber. That calls for a pity party if ever a situation does."

"I'll admit it's not encouraging. The dumb blonde cheerleader cliché was invented by those two, after all. But, hey, they were hot."

Andrea simply narrowed her eyes.

"And clearly hotness clouds the male mind, since Tyler didn't remember that nobody was less likely to know anything about island history than Lana and Amber."

"Clearly."

Any minute now she was going to say the wrong thing, and he'd know who she was, or somebody was going to recognize her—she'd been back to the island for nearly six months, after all. Or, even worse, she was going to launch into an explanation of South Carolina's role in every conflict since the War of Independence.

With a sigh, she pulled off her mask.

"Oh, no, you don't." Sloan snatched the mask, then slid it back over Andrea's head. "We just need to adjust our plan. You need action, not talk."

TYLER STOOD IN THE PARLOR alone.

He was surrounded by partygoers, his fellow islanders, many of them friends. But the one person he wanted to see was nowhere around.

He'd just met her. Talked to her for less than ten minutes. Indulged in the alluring scent of citrus and sea clinging to her skin for mere seconds. And yet he couldn't help his gaze from continually darting around the room, desperate for the sight of her.

When he saw Sloan, he strode toward her. "Hey, have you seen " He trailed off. How idiotic was he to have not gotten his mystery woman's name?

"Your lady in blue?" Sloan asked.

Something in his stomach leaped. "Yeah."

"She was feeling a bit hot. She stepped outside to get some air."

As Sloan turned away, he snagged her arm. "You know her, huh?"

She smiled. "I do."

Then she turned and began chatting with a couple a few feet away.

Women. They were a damnable confusing species.

But still beautiful, stimulating, intriguing, soft, inviting and impossible to live without. At least for him.

What the hell was he doing, thinking about all this while a superhot blonde was outside, presumably alone, getting air?

As quickly and discreetly as possible, he weaved his way around his—hopefully—future constituents, darted into the kitchen and exited the back door.

He breathed in the scent of salty sea air while he scanned the backyard for his mystery lady.

Beyond an ancient oak, a group of palms surrounded a white wooden gazebo lit by three spotlights staked in the grass. A shadowed figure stood inside the structure.

As atmospheres went, it was pretty damn near perfect.

After straightening his tie, he headed across the lawn. She stood with her back to him but turned as he approached. The lacy, black-and-blue mask still covered the upper half of her face, so her pale green eyes stood out in stark contrast as they watched him intently.

"It's very Old South, meeting this way, don't you think?"

"Whatever are you suggesting, sir?" she asked in an exaggerated drawl as she fluttered her lashes.

He stepped so close he could swear he felt her heart beating against her chest. "Anything you want."

"But I might ask for more than you're willing to give."

"I don't see how."

Their gazes held for a long moment, then she grasped his hand and led him to the beach seat on one side of the gazebo.

He glanced down at their joined hands and for once felt incapable of saying something charming and clever. "The party's nice, huh?"

"Sloan's a pro at socializing."

"That she is. Have you known her long?"

She smiled as if she knew he was trying to get more information about her. "Awhile."

"And Aidan seems like a great guy. He'd have to be pretty steely to get past the scrutiny of Sheriff Caldwell."

"He is. You must be rather sturdy yourself to risk following in his legendary shoes. Or, in his case, boots."

He shrugged. He'd never lacked confidence in his ability to lead before; he wished he didn't now. "We'll see, I guess." He slid his thumb across the back of her hand. "Do you have to wear the mask?"

"Yes," she said, seemingly unfazed by his quick conversation change.

"Why?"

"I'm shy." Though she leaned closer, belying her words. Her gaze dropped, quite deliberately, to his lips. "Did you really come out here to talk?"

He had actually, but only because he'd sensed she was a woman who could carry on a conversation easily and not the type for groping strangers. Still, he was a man, so his heartbeat picked up speed, anticipation flowed through his veins and...

And why the hell had he, again, lapsed into musing when faced with—

Before he could finish the thought, her lips were on his.

Cupping her cheek in his hand, he angled his head and deepened the kiss. Her mouth was soft, responsive, eager and seductive. Her pulse pounded beneath his fingers. Her scent, sweet and intoxicating, drew him under her spell, forcing the rest of the world away.

His desire to have her only intensified with this first, intimate touch. Tasting her, he knew he wanted more. He wanted all.

3

ANDREA CLENCHED HER hand around Tyler's thigh.

Dazzling, almost magical sensations bounced along her pulse points like a pinball machine after a tilt.

How was it possible that the reality was even better than over a decade of fantasies? That she could change the mistakes and regrets of the past with one touch?

And as suddenly as those realizations crashed over her, she also knew something was wrong. There should be feelings, not just urges. She should want him for more than just to prove he shouldn't have rejected her before. They should talk or date or—

His tongue tangled with hers, and her desire soared up in yet another thrilling spike.

Okay, maybe not completely wrong.

He trailed his lips down her neck. "This is crazy."

"Yeah." She gasped as his tongue flicked against her ear. "Do that again."

He did. He also wrapped his arm around her waist and molded her against him. Her heart thundered along with his. How different this was from the first, and only, kiss they'd shared. When she'd felt awkward, and he'd been uncomfortable.

They fit together now like puzzle pieces always meant to link.

His hand moved up her body to cup her breast, his thumb flicking over her nipple, which pushed tautly against the dress's thick silken fabric.

Her stomach clenched. Heat flooded her body. "We can't do this here," she gasped.

"You're right. I—" He kissed her again, firmly, then pulled back. "We have to stop."

"Stop?" She wrapped her hand around his neck and urged him toward her. "Who said anything about stopping? We just have to go somewhere else."

Her breathing was coming in pants; she didn't want to move away from him, give either of them a chance to question the maddening need that had overtaken them.

But neither did she want an audience.

"Come with me," she whispered against his lips.

She slid her hand down his arm, feeling the ripple of muscles beneath his formal wear. *Hang on, girl. Try to think.* While reciting the periodic table in her head, she linked their hands and led him out of the gazebo and into the house. They darted up the back staircase from the kitchen to her room on the second floor.

After finding condoms in the bedside table—*thank you, Sloan*—they shed their clothes with fevered haste. His body seemed to consist of endless miles of lean, masculine muscle just begging for her to explore, and the way his lustful gaze raced over her body, she was grateful she'd taken up morning beach runs as exercise.

She left the mask on; he didn't seem to mind. It wasn't until they fell naked and kissing onto the bed that Andrea's overstimulated mind acknowledged her fantasy was really coming true.

Tyler Landry was looking at her as if she was the most

beautiful woman on the planet. He was touching her, kissing her. He wanted her.

"I can't believe this is happening," he whispered against her throat as if he knew her thoughts. "There are fifty people having a party downstairs."

She closed her eyes and arched her back, absorbing the delicious sensation of his lips on her flushed skin. "I don't like crowds."

His hand cupped her breast, his thumb flicking over her nipple. "At this moment, neither do I."

Her hips jerked as need raced down her spine. She gripped his shoulders, her fingernails digging into the muscles. She wanted to say things, to tell him how amazing she felt, but she feared giving too much of herself away. Instead, she absorbed the pleasure in silence, her heart's frantic hammering the only betrayal of how special the moment really was.

When he slid his hand between her legs, she gasped. Her body clenched around his exploring fingers. She had a vague thought about stroking him, feeling the evidence of his desire, but she couldn't seem to put the idea into action.

He stopped the incredible, deliberately stimulating movements only long enough to put on protection, then his body was between her legs, his erection poised at the entrance to her body. "Hey," he said quietly, his hand gliding across her cheek, "open your eyes."

When she did, she found his lovely blue eyes focused intimately and tenderly on hers, and for some ridiculous reason, tears gathered in her throat.

Something like recognition jumped into his eyes briefly, but it was gone before she was sure she'd seen it at all. He said nothing. He simply slid the pad of his thumb across her bottom lip, then, as he kissed her, he pushed inside her. His hardness filled her, and she moaned with satisfaction.

Though that sensation didn't last long.

As he began to move, and their hips found a synchronized rhythm, the tension of desire tightened. Satisfaction spiraled away, replaced by a desperate hunger for completion. A need for more. Faster, harder, stronger.

The jerk of her climax, when it finally broke, made her cry out in surprise. The pulsing sparks that followed and spread outward to affect every inch of her body were extraordinary, something she'd never before experienced with any lover.

Suddenly, she knew she was in trouble. That once wouldn't be enough. One night couldn't be all they ever had.

And she wasn't, in any way, shape or form, over him.

TYLER HAD NO IDEA how long his phone had been ringing when he finally emerged from his comalike sleep and groped along the nightstand to silence the irritating sound.

"Tyler, it's Sheriff Caldwell."

"Yeah?" He yawned. The sheriff's normally commanding voice sounded far away. "Y-yes, sir."

"You're not still in bed, are ya? It's eight o'clock."

"Uh, I— Uh…"

"No more cushy hours for you, boy! This is law enforcement. We don't sleep."

Eyes still closed, Tyler rubbed his temple. "I know what dawn looks like, Sheriff. I was in the Navy."

The sheriff snorted. "Sissies."

"The Marines."

"Cocky sissies."

"Are you serious, or is that a ploy to get me up faster?"

"I don't do ploys, son."

With a sudden image of the sheriff—six feet six inches, even without the Stetson, shoulders as broad as an aircraft carrier and piercing blue eyes—Tyler blinked. He tried to remember where he was and recalled immediately he was naked in an unfamiliar bed. But a somehow familiar scent lingered in the air. *Her* scent.

He bolted upright.

She was gone. Hell.

Memories of the impulsive, carnal night flooded him, bringing a physical reaction to various parts of his body. He recalled his mystery lady's slim, athletic body, her inviting smile, her moans of pleasure mingling with his.

At one point, he'd finally convinced her to take off the mask, but only with the lights off. He'd wondered if she had a scar on her cheek or near her eye that she was self-conscious about, but he'd been pretty intimate with her skin throughout the night, and he hadn't felt one.

So why the mystery? Did she have anonymous sex with strangers often?

No, wait. Not strangers. She'd said they'd met before. How? When?

"I need your help," the sheriff said, yanking Tyler back to reality—and the job he was supposed to be focusing on. "Dwayne just called me in a panic."

"Burris?" Other than his fear of gunfire, Dwayne was a pretty easygoing, if not incredibly experienced, fellow deputy. "Is he okay?"

"Besides having to breathe in a paper bag to deal with his anxiety attack, I expect so. He's over at old Mrs. Jackson's house. Seems her silver tea set is missing. Stolen, according to her."

Tyler had an immediate recollection of a tiny, gray-haired woman who lived alone in an enormous beach house with half a dozen fluffy show dogs and was notorious for flirting like a teenager with every man on the island. "You mean that old lady at the south end of Beach Road with the dogs? She's got to be a hundred by now."

"Ninety-three last June," the sheriff confirmed. "If you remember her, I'm guessin' you also know she claims to be a descendant of President Andrew Jackson."

"Claims? I thought she was."

"I expect she is. Don't know for sure. But when you've got that much money, son, very few people argue with you."

"I guess so."

"I'm makin' this distinction because you should never take anything on word only in an investigation. Legends on this island are as plentiful as gossip. Retold so often, it's hard to pry apart truth and fiction."

Recognizing the admonition was Buddy's way of imparting advice, Tyler responded with a polite, "Yes, sir."

"The missing or stolen tea service was apparently the president's favorite. He even took it with him during his years in Washington. She's pretty insistent about gettin' it back."

"I imagine it's valuable."

"To her and the rest of the island." He cleared his throat. "My daughter will be bending my ear about the historical significance as soon as she hears—and you can bet Mrs. Jackson is already on the phone to her. Dwayne is okay and all—once he stops hyperventilatin'—but he's not exactly Perry Mason. And I'm in Bermuda. What am I supposed to do about any of it?"

"Nothing, Sheriff. That's what I'm here for, right?"

"You bet your ass you are. Hang on." Even though the

sheriff must have covered the phone receiver, Tyler could hear muffled voices—one of them distinctly female. "Sorry about that," Buddy said when he returned. "It sure couldn't hurt your campaign to solve a sentimental problem like this one so close to the election."

"I'll alert the papers." And despite the issues of the night before still yet to deal with, Tyler found himself intrigued by the case. It had to be more interesting than rosebush vandalism. "You said *missing* or stolen. You doubt the theft?"

There was a brief pause. "See there, knew you'd make a good sheriff. And, yeah, I got plenty of doubt about the theft. With the owner's advanced age and general dottiness, who knows where the tea set really is. The old lady could even have her mind on insurance fraud."

"But she's loaded."

"She's also a troublemaker. Walk careful with her, you hear?"

"I will. And don't worry about any of this. I can handle it."

"As long as you get plenty of rest."

Tyler wasn't about to admit he'd slept in because he hadn't slept during the night. "As long as," he said, though he knew he'd never live down the assumed laziness. "How's Mabel?" It was common, but as yet unconfirmed knowledge that the sheriff was vacationing with the local café owner, whom he'd been dating the last several months.

Clearly annoyed, the sheriff snorted. "How should I know? I'm on a fishin' trip. Solve this case, Lieutenant. And quickly. Or your Navy rank may be the last title you ever have."

He hung up.

Tyler flopped back on the pillows, staring at the room's high ceiling. Yesterday, he was going through the motions of the election and, really, his life as a whole. He'd retired from active duty as advised by his commander. He'd reconnected with his family. He'd come home to the island to begin a new career. To remember what he'd gone off to fight for in the first place.

But he hadn't felt more than a glimmer of satisfaction from any of the changes. He'd questioned his decision over and over. He'd loved his life in the military. Did he really belong back home? Could he adapt to civilian life again?

And now, barely twenty-four hours later, he had a case to fill his days and a woman who could fill his nights.

If he could find her.

Flinging the sheets aside, he let his feet drop to the floor beside the bed. He vaguely remembered taking off his watch and setting it on the bedside table near his phone. Glancing in that direction, he saw the gold-and-platinum watch given to him by his grandfather lying there. As he snatched it up, he noticed a white business card beneath.

Andrea Hastings, Appraiser.

Just like when the sheriff mentioned Mrs. Jackson's name, a mental picture flooded Tyler's mind. Dark blond hair, braces, glasses with a thick black rim, math genius, shy smile.

No. No way. *She couldn't be.*

Another memory zipped into focus. This scene had taken place on the beach, late at night just before he'd left for basic training, in the shadows of a palmetto bush.

His shy math tutor's unusual, pale green, fairylike eyes, somewhat blurry behind her glasses, had focused on his face as she'd told him about the crush she'd cherished for years. How she'd known he'd recently broken off his two-year relationship with his girlfriend, who was angry about him joining the Navy instead of him taking any of the walk-on offers from several universities to join their football team.

Then she—Andrea, the smartest, kindest person he'd ever known—had kissed him.

He'd been kind in return, explaining his need to serve his country, as everyone in his family had done before him. And, maybe, as he really concentrated on the memory, he'd been tempted to find out what might happen between them if school, future plans and social barriers hadn't been in the way.

But he'd said nothing of this brief spark of interest to her at the time. He'd smiled and set her aside, all but patted her head as he set off to bigger and better glories.

Fast forward to last night.

The moment he'd fitted his body between the welcoming hips of his mystery woman, when he'd asked her to open her eyes and he'd seen the familiar—though he hadn't recognized them at the time—fairy eyes.

He braced his arms on his thighs, still holding the business card between his fingers. *What have I done?*

It all made sense—having met her before, her knowing Sloan, her intelligent, witty comments, even her reluctance to remove her mask.

Regret clenched his gut as he forced himself to flip the card over, knowing, just knowing, there would be a note.

Second time's the charm.

"Yeah. I guess so."

He glanced back at the card and noticed an address on Beach Road and phone number. The address wasn't for an office, though. The house number was too high. That end of the street contained only homes. Big, expensive, ocean-front homes.

Andrea had apparently put her formidable brains to successful use.

No surprise there. But the address also meant she was only a few blocks down from his new case. After handling Mrs. Jackson and calming Dwayne, he had another stop to make and an apology to impart, one that was several years overdue.

As soon as he had it out with that little instigator Sloan.

There was no way sweet Andrea Hastings had come up with seduction and a secret identity on her own.

After tossing on his rumpled clothes, he headed down-stairs, where he heard voices coming from the kitchen. Sloan was sitting on her husband's lap while he laughed and tried to hold a coffee mug out of her reach.

Normally, he would have slipped out of the house and let them "play," but he wasn't going to let any more time than absolutely necessary come between him and making things right with Andrea.

"Sorry to interrupt, but we have to talk," he said as he approached the table.

Sloan glanced over her shoulder at him. Her expression was carefully blank. "About what?"

"Not what." He held up Andrea's card. "Who."

"I'M A SLUT," ANDREA said miserably when she opened the door to Sloan's knock.

Sloan sighed. "Oh, good grief."

"I am." Trudging back into the den, Andrea flopped on the sofa and didn't even stop to admire the view from the window-dominated back wall of her house. The sight of her much-treasured kitchen and sunroom, the waves crashing on the shore mere yards away, always reminded her of how far she'd come, how hard she'd worked for her success.

She threw a cold washcloth over her face to counteract her flaming, guilty cheeks. "I slept with a man I never intend to see again. I had sex with him to deal with *my* emotional issues and shortcomings, never once wondering if he was ready to take that intimate step so quickly."

"You feel guilty for last night?" Sloan's surprise was clear.

Lifting the washcloth, Andrea peeked at her friend. "Shouldn't I?"

"No." Sloan—dressed in a professional, but somehow still alluring, pale pink suit and hot silver sandals—settled into the nearby chair, crossed her long, tan legs and stared at Andrea. "You had a decent orgasm, didn't you?"

She swallowed hard. "Beyond decent, and several."

"And you fulfilled your fantasy to see Tyler Landry naked."

"The reality was better."

"So you successfully seduced your fantasy man, which was better than you imagined it would be, you regained your confidence as a desirable woman, plus you got revenge for all the crappy, selfish guys who've flooded the land for the last two thousand years and used women the same way." Sloan leaned back in her chair. "What's the guilt about? Do you think he would have hung around all night if he felt used and didn't want to be with you again? And again?" She paused, her mouth tipping up. "Many, many times over?"

"I guess not," Andrea said, considering the sense in her friend's words. Tyler was a great many things but gullible wasn't one of them. "But still—"

"So you really never want to see him again?"

"That was the plan, if you remember. The plan you sold me on as you tied me into that breath-stealing costume. Get over my teenage fantasy issues, my awkward past, try not to focus on my convicted-felon-now-on-probation brother and move on to…" Andrea jolted to her feet. Her heart pounded in a panicked rush. "This is *your* fault. You knew this would happen."

"What?" Sloan asked, blinking with fake innocence.

"Me, getting hooked on him again."

"I didn't think you'd be satisfied with one night," she admitted. "So, why does it have to be one? Why can't you see him again?"

"Because it's all wrong! I lied. I wore a mask, for pity's sake."

Sloan's gaze grew speculative. "Even during…?" She waved her hand when Andrea shook her head, unwilling to spill intimate details. "And you didn't lie. You were mysterious and intriguing. Obviously, it worked."

"But I'm *not* mysterious and intriguing."

"So see him again and be you. What's the worst that could happen?"

She headed out.

Feeling ridiculous but unable to stifle the urge, Andrea followed. "Did you see him when he left this morning?"

"Yep."

"How did he seem?"

"Annoyed, confused and anxious." She paused at the door. "Of course the last thing could be because my father called."

"About what?"

"Some case," Sloan said vaguely. "Anyway, Tyler showed

me your card—nice touch, by the way—and said we had to talk."

"How mad is he?"

"He isn't thrilled with me. You, he's crazy about."

Andrea's traitorous, susceptible heart jumped.

Sloan's lips twitched. "And *he* seemed to think the mask was sexy."

"What else did he say?"

"He wanted to know what you've been doing the last twelve years. I told him he had to find out for himself."

"What else did he say?"

Turning as she stood on the porch, Sloan shrugged. "You aren't in high school anymore, you know." Then her gaze raked Andrea's ratty sweatpants and paint-stained tank top. "Put on some makeup and decent clothes and stop wallowing. You're supposed to be floating on a cloud with blissful, lustful memories keeping you airborne."

"Yeah, I'll work on that."

"You might want to work fast. Mrs. Jackson's silver tea service is missing, so Tyler's just a few doors away, investigating the case. That's what my dad called about this morning. So, unless I'm completely off base—and I rarely am—he's going to come by here." With a sassy wave, she scooted off the porch. "Have fun."

Andrea's jaw dropped. She watched her—supposedly—best friend swing her purse and her hips into her cute little convertible as if she didn't have a care in the world. "You could've led with that!" she shouted after her.

"MRS. JACKSON, ARE YOU *sure* you locked the china cabinet last night?" Tyler asked his, hopefully, future constituent.

Henrietta Delmar Jackson peered at him from behind

tiny, silver-framed glasses. "Of course I'm sure, honey." Her veiny hand clutched Tyler's. "Are you sure that girlfriend of yours wouldn't mind if you got a little side action?"

Deputy Dwayne lifted his paper bag—already well-used since arriving at the Jackson home—back to his face and inhaled deeply. Dwayne was a nice guy, but actual crime scared him. He was more of a behind-the-scenes person.

Glaring at his colleague, who sat beside him on the uncomfortable, but no doubt valuable, antique sofa in Mrs. Jackson's front parlor, Tyler fought desperately to keep his attention on the investigation.

Such as it was.

He'd been forced to lie about having a girlfriend to keep the ninety-something "victim" from crawling into his lap. All he needed was paramedics arriving to save Dwayne from himself and Tyler from Mrs. Jackson, and his humiliation would be complete and forever.

"But the lock wasn't forced," Tyler continued. "Neither were any of the doors to the house."

"I've seen those paranormal shows on TV," Mrs. Jackson said with a defiant nod. "They could zip in here with a blink."

"They?"

"The aliens."

Mere weeks ago his life was a mix of foreign lands, missions in the dead of night, glimmers of hope, fighting to avoid dwelling on fear and loneliness. Today, aliens and zipping—whatever that was. Did he prefer reality or ridiculousness?

"What was I saying?"

"They could zip with a blink."

"Right." She nodded. "The aliens obviously zipped in here and stole my precious silver. They need it for their weapons of mass destruction, you see."

"Yeah," Tyler said, looking at Dwayne, who shrugged, the paper bag still over his mouth and nose. "I bet they do."

"But if aliens weren't responsible," Tyler continued to Mrs. Jackson, "does anyone else—on this planet—have a key to your house?"

She narrowed her bleary eyes. "Are you mocking me, young man?"

"No, ma'am." And he thanked God she wasn't still calling him *honey.* "I'm going to find your silver service."

"Sheriff Caldwell could find it faster," she said.

"I'm sure he could. But Deputy Burris and I are on duty at the moment." He nudged Dwayne in the ribs, forcing him to lower the paper bag he'd been breathing into. "Aren't we?"

"Yes, sir," Dwayne parroted.

No help there. Great. "We'll look around the property and dust for fingerprints, Mrs. Jackson," Tyler said as he rose. "But it would be helpful if you could let us know about the key and give us a list of all your employees and anybody who's recently shown an interest in your tea set."

Her eyes brightened. "Are you going to turn out the lights and make things turn blue like that cute boy on *CSI?*"

Since those blue lights tended to reveal blood splatters, Tyler certainly hoped not.

He and Dwayne spent the next hour searching the house and property for the tea set without success. The lack of results frustrated Tyler in a big way, since he'd expected to find the missing item under a bed or table, hidden from enemies of the alien persuasion. But, true to his word, he dutifully covered the table where the tea set normally rested with fingerprint powder, lifted several viable prints and knew they'd all wind up belonging to Miss Jackson, her friends or her employees.

By the time he and Dwayne escaped to the porch, thoughts of his personal problems and lack of sleep had caught up with him, leaving him tired and even more annoyed.

"Well, it's not there," he said to Dwayne as they headed to their respective cars.

"Unless she buried it in the backyard."

For the first time since waking up naked in a twist of sheets without a hot woman anywhere in sight, Tyler smiled. "There's a viable possibility. Beyond that, there's no forced entry. No footprints. No enemies—on Earth, anyway. Let's look at the cleaning staff, the pool boy, anybody who has access to the house on a regular basis."

"The church ladies might bring her meals. It seems I've heard Sister Mary Katherine talk about that recently."

"But the church ladies—and the good Sister in particular—aren't involved in a theft, so it's likely somebody she employed ran off with the silver, hoping for a fast payoff. I doubt it's a professional, because even if he knew the sig nificance of the set and its worth, a smart thief wouldn't touch something that hot. Some pawnshop owner's about to get more than he's bargaining for, then this whole thing is going to get sticky."

Dwayne nodded. "Yes, sir."

"Don't call me sir, Dwayne. We're the same rank."

"But when you're sheriff…"

"*If* I'm sheriff. Mrs. Jackson may be the abrupt, crash-landing of my campaign." And, dammit, he couldn't even find the energy to care about his career or the silver-stealing silliness. He wanted to see Andrea and apologize, clarify, then repeat last night. "I'll check with area pawn-shops. Let's close this down before it gets out and every-body's talking about crime running rampant without Buddy here to keep order."

Smiling, Dwayne saluted. "You got it, boss."

"Don't salute me, Dwayne."

"Even when you're sheriff?"

"Even then."

4

"ARE YOU GOING TO invite me in?"

Andrea stared at Tyler, standing on her front porch, a half smile on his sculpted face. He wore faded jeans and a white collared shirt. A gold star—that she somehow found both adorable and sexy—was pinned over his heart.

"I— Well…sure." Stepping back, she ran a self-conscious hand over her ponytail. After Sloan's desertion, she'd dressed in coordinating clothes and hastily used the straightening iron and some balm to calm the sea-air frizzies that had taken over her hair. Still, she knew she looked nothing like the mysterious woman in blue from the night before.

It was a wonder he'd recognized her.

"The house is beautiful," he said, glancing around the foyer while she closed the door. "Yours?"

"Uh-huh." She cleared her throat and tried to banish the image of him the last time she'd seen him, naked and well-satisfied. "I bought it when I moved back a few months ago."

His gaze connected with hers. "Business must be good."

"Yeah."

"I guess you have a great view of the ocean. That's one thing I really miss about leaving the Navy."

"Do you? I'm sorry about last night," she blurted.

His grin widened. "I'm not."

Responding as always to his perfect smile, her heart pounded, not realizing hope was lost. "But you have to be angry. I tricked you."

"And I want to know why. But I'm not mad."

She waited for him to change his mind. But he said nothing more. He just looked at her expectantly.

He was *supposed* to be angry. Feel indignation over her deceit. Yell. Then, she could go back to consulting, fixing her house and making sure her brother didn't break his probation. There was no future for her and Tyler. Their chemistry had been a charade.

"Okay," she said finally. "If you want, we could sit on the deck and…talk." She turned and headed across the polished wooden floors through the den, which, along with the kitchen, dominated the back of the house. A long, curved bar separated the two rooms, and she winced at the scattered paint samples littering its black granite surface. Given her normally meticulous nature, this was a sign of how off balance and distracted she'd been all day.

She took one bracing glance at the rippling waves in the distance, then sat on the end of the red-and-blue-striped cushions on the chaise, leaving Tyler the matching wicker sofa. "So…the thing is…"

"You were very clever last night."

She smiled. "Some things never change."

His gaze roved her body. "Some things have."

"I guess I'm a late bloomer."

"So brains and beauty now, is it? Not that you weren't cute before."

"I wasn't even in cute's neighborhood."

"Sure you were. There was something really great about your eyes. I noticed it last night, too. Though I didn't connect you with…well, you. What'd you do about the glasses?"

"LASIK surgery," she said slowly, struck a bit dumb by the *great about your eyes* comment. He'd noticed her eyes? "Would you have…responded the same way if you'd known who I was last night?"

"I guess so. Why would it matter?"

She worried her lower lip and forced herself to look directly at him. "Look, to be frank, I acted pretty impulsively last night. I've been working a lot, and I haven't—"

"What do you do?"

"As an insurance appraiser, I mostly investigate frauds and historical forgeries."

He looked impressed. "Yeah?"

"It has its moments. But the thing is, I haven't taken the time to get involved with anyone for a while."

"When was the last time you'd had sex before last night?"

"I—" Talk about frank. She blinked. "I'm not sure."

"Maybe I should have clarified—when's the last time you had great sex?"

Never without you.

The uncensored thought, thankfully, popped in her head, not out of her mouth. Was that really true? She didn't want to pause and wonder because then she'd be in serious trouble. "Could I please get this out?"

He leaned back into the sofa cushions. "Sorry. Go ahead."

"So I had this unresolved fantasy about you." When he opened his mouth, she held up her finger. She'd like to get this done with as little humiliation as possible. "Not that I've spent the last decade pining over your yearbook picture or anything. I just felt…unresolved about us. I mean, I kissed you, you said *no thanks* and that was that, but I still wondered. And hoped things might be different."

She rose and turned partly away from him. Offering the truth this way was uncomfortable. In all but the most basic sense, he was a stranger. "When I found out you were back on the island, I avoided you. I didn't want to remember how it used to be." How it felt to want him and not be able to have him. Drawing a deep breath, she pushed on. "Then last night, Sloan and I got carried away talking about regrets."

"And fantasies?"

She glanced at him over her shoulder, noting he wasn't smiling anymore. He'd gone very still. "And fantasies. You were mine."

"Were?"

"Sure. Last night lived up to—well…really surpassed—all my expectations."

"So now that you're satisfied, so to speak, you're done with me?"

Wow, that sounded cold. And she supposed she had to face up to the fact that she had been. "It wasn't mature or honest of me, I know. I am sorry." She sank onto the lounge chair, laying her hand on top of his. "If I'd handled things differently, I guess we might have been friends."

"Friends, huh?"

She couldn't sense his mood, but he hadn't stormed out. Yet. She'd used him for sex. He got that, right? "Well, if you want to try, I guess we could start over."

"Will us being friends involve you patting my hand?"

She glanced over, where her hand covered his. "If you need me to."

For the first time, he looked annoyed. "Then I'll pass."

She started to draw her hand back, but he surprised her by wrapping his fingers around her wrist, and with that little bit of pressure he was able to unbalance her, so she landed in his lap.

Before she could do more than suck in a surprised breath, his mouth had covered hers. With his hand behind her neck, he angled her head, deepening the kiss, sliding his tongue against hers, heat pumping off his body like a furnace.

The sensual hunger that had fed them through the night burst to life with a craving intensity she was sure she'd never escape.

And why would she want to go?

His need for her and her longing for him were explosive chemical compounds, undiscovered until last evening. Impulsiveness and a mask of deceit had led to something magical, something she'd been sure would never strike again. So she reveled in the recurrence.

When he released her, she was panting. "Are you crazy? What was that about?"

"I was just demonstrating that I don't want to be friends."

"Okay." She nodded, but her ears were still ringing, so she was pretty sure she'd misheard him.

"I'm glad you agree."

"Agree about what?"

"Not being friends. We've moved past the friend stage, don't you think? I would have rather you told me about your fantasy to start with, but I'm willing to catch up. Which one would you like to do next?"

Do what?

He wanted to know about her fantasies and act them out? "I think I just fell into one," she muttered.

He waggled his eyebrows. "Sex on the beach, huh?

That's a personal favorite of mine, too. We should probably wait until after dark, but if you're game…" He levered them to standing, still holding her in his arms. "I could always arrest us afterward."

She kicked her legs. He'd lost his mind. "Put me down."

"Here or out there?" He bobbed his head toward the ocean.

"I could probably use a good dunking, but here's good," she told him. Standing, she had to brace her hand against his chest in order to get her bearings. His kissing ought to qualify the man as a lethal weapon. "We need to clarify some things."

He looked amused. "More talking, huh? I prefer action."

"Yes, I—" She stopped as the power of those potent baby blues twisted her stomach into a knot of desire. "I kind of figured that. But I feel compelled to point out that I used you for sex."

"And anytime you want to do it again, I'm available."

"But I don't do that." His wicked grin called her a liar. "Okay, I don't normally do that."

"Good to know I'm a special case."

But I don't want you to be special, she nearly blurted out. "I date men," she said instead. "I have relationships with them. I don't have casual sex." And if that tidbit didn't send him running, nothing would.

"No kidding? Me, too. Well, not the part about men. How about I pick you up for dinner at seven?"

"We can't date."

"Sure we can. You said a few minutes ago you weren't involved with anybody."

"But—" She certainly didn't belong with him—island heartthrob, local hero, star of her erotic fantasies.

Their relationship, such as it was, had started off all

wrong. Even if she set aside the humiliation of the old crush, him knowing about the fantasy stuff and the way they'd rapidly reacquainted themselves with each other, their compatibility in bed was all they had. Since that was a small aspect—well, maybe not small, but not the be-all, end-all, either—of a successful relationship, she didn't see any reason to pursue an ultimately futile project.

Plus, she just plain didn't like that he'd breezed into her house, kissed her, then asked her out as if dinner, a little wine and her flat on her back were all a foregone conclusion.

Of course last night she'd wound up on her back without any dinner at all.

But then it had been all her idea.

"I already have dinner plans," she said, crossing her arms over her chest. They were with her brother, but still.

"You do?"

He clearly hadn't expected this. No woman had probably ever turned him down. It was yet another reason anything between them was doomed. The balance would always be weighted on his side. She, like everyone else, would always be a little in awe, and she couldn't let herself be that vulnerable to him again.

"I do appreciate you coming by and clearing the air, but I have work to do this afternoon," she said, "so if you don't mind…" And she extended her arm toward the door leading from the deck to the house.

"You're throwing me out?"

She opened the door, holding it wide. "I'm showing you out."

He stared at her a long moment, then smiled and moved toward her.

She had a second to recognize this was the identical, ultraconfident, Vote For Me smile that graced signs all over the island, before his scent and nearness overwhelmed her and her brain went fuzzy.

"If your date doesn't go well, you can always call me later."

The cockiness wasn't working on her today. Well, actually it was, but he didn't have to know that. "I'm sure my date will be more than entertaining."

He slid his thumb across her cheek. "Too bad."

"Oh, so you're not going to hang around and fight him for me?"

"Would I win?"

She thought of her quiet, gangly, video-game-loving brother. He was crafty, not brawny. "Probably," she hedged.

"It's tempting. Winning you, I mean, not the fight itself."

"But…"

"I've already seen more fighting than I need."

His years in the military hadn't been all medals and glory, it seemed. And, despite her vow to get him out of her life, she found herself curious about the shadows that had moved into his eyes.

"And the islanders might not appreciate their would-be sheriff picking a fight," he added.

"I guess so."

He moved past her, then crossed through the den. She followed him down the hall, wishing she could close her eyes and block the view of his fitted jeans riding his narrow hips.

He turned. Regret filled his gorgeous eyes. "Call me if you change your mind."

She forced a smile and steeled her resolve. "Okay." As she also forced herself to close the door behind him, she came to an honest and disturbing conclusion.

Despite all her denials, delusional pep talks and hopes to the contrary, their chemistry was no charade.

"SIR, YOU HAVE A visitor," Dwayne said, sticking his head around the door frame the next morning.

It was Monday, but Tyler resisted the urge to sigh. Barely. "Please don't call me sir, Dwayne."

"But you're in *his* office," Dwayne said, a hint of awed fear in his voice. "Sitting at *his* desk."

"And when he comes back, give him all the sirs he can handle."

"Lester Cradock said that if he wins the election for sheriff, I'll get my own bullwhip, but I have to address him as the Grand Island Pouba."

"Then you'd better vote for me. Who's here?"

"Sir—" He cleared his throat. "I mean who's where?"

"The visitor, Dwayne."

"Sister Mary Katherine."

Now Tyler did wince. "Did she say what she needs?"

"No. Sorry. Should I have asked her?"

Rising, Tyler shook his head. "You're not my secretary." He dropped a pile of faxes on the desk as he headed out of the office. "I'm not getting anywhere on this missing-silver case anyway. Nothing about the theft makes any sense."

"Yesterday you seemed sure the tea set would turn up in the pawnshops."

"Proving I know significantly less about local law enforcement than I do about flying M-16s."

"I'm not sure I'd put that on your campaign posters."

"You're probably right."

Would he have a stronger focus on this case if he wasn't spending every waking moment thinking about Andrea? If he hadn't slept wishing Andrea was beside him? If he couldn't swear the alluring scent of her perfume brushed past him every five minutes?

He could admit his ego was bruised. But the feeling weighing in his chest went beyond ego and disappointment. He was hurt.

He rarely had trouble getting and keeping a woman's attention. Where had he gone wrong with Andrea? Was one night really enough for her? She wasn't involved with anybody, but she'd had dinner plans she couldn't—or wouldn't—change to be with him.

At some point, he really needed to look around for his charm.

"Have you heard back from Mrs. Jackson's pool cleaning company yet?" he asked Dwayne as they walked down the hall.

"I don't know how much of a company it is, boss. And his answering machine's message is *Went to catch some waves. Later.* So we might not hear from him right on through the end of summer."

"Keep trying, will you? Maybe we'll go by his office this afternoon and see if any of his neighbors have seen him."

"I think he lives and works from his parents' garage."

"Terrific. Maybe they know where he is."

They rounded the corner into the outer office, which separated the rest of the station from the waiting area. For security purposes, the room had a large front window made of bulletproof glass.

Aqua Joliet, the station's day receptionist and 911 dispatcher, sat leaning back in her chair, her bare feet propped on her desk as she smacked gum and flipped through the pages of a fashion magazine.

This was her usual pose, and since Tyler was only temporarily in charge and he'd yet to find any fault with her job performance—even the lack of footwear could be considered normal for the island—he didn't generally comment. But with Sister Mary Katherine sitting only yards away, dressed in her formal black-and-white habit and knitting something, the whole business seemed strange at best, disrespectful at worst.

He stopped at her desk and leaned toward her. "If crime were running rampant on the island, Aqua, and your fellow citizens were to dial nine-one-one, would they get an analysis of London Sheraton's latest party dress or actual help from the sheriff's department?"

Blowing a bubble, Aqua tucked a blue-and-blond-streaked lock of hair behind her ear. Which actually didn't turn out to be either a nervous or defiant gesture. With her hair out of the way, Tyler could see a small earphone, presumably linked to the phone system on her desk. "Should I be concerned about a crime spree, Lieutenant?" She flipped another page in the magazine. "And London Sheraton's taste sucks. There's nothing to discuss."

Clearly, he'd lost both his charm and his ability to command.

Planting a firm smile on his face, he opened the outer office door, then headed toward the nun. "Sister, let's go back to my—uh…the sheriff's office."

She rose, her pale, smooth face wrinkling briefly in a smile. "Thank you, Tyler. I missed you in church on Sunday."

He didn't think telling the sister that he'd crawled out of a strange bed after a particularly lascivious night was the right tone for their conversation. "Yes, ma'am. I'll make a stronger effort this week."

In the office, he offered her one of the chairs in front of the sheriff's battered oak desk, then sat behind it. She tucked her knitting in her tote bag and folded her hands in her lap.

"I think you know why I'm here," she said.

A flash of Andrea, flushed and naked, scooted through his memory. He staunchly blocked out the image. "No, Sister, I'm sorry. I really don't."

"Henrietta called me."

"I see."

"It's vital this case be solved."

"My team and I are working very hard to make that happen."

"Your team?" The sister smiled—benevolently even. "You, Deputy Dwayne and Miss Aqua."

She wasn't both the spiritual leader and crab-claw-edged spine of the island for nothing.

"Yes, Sister. My team and I are confident we'll find the perpetrator. I've interviewed Mrs. Jackson, searched her house and dusted for fingerprints. I'm working my way through interviews of everyone who's had recent access to her house. I've talked to or gotten faxes from practically every pawnshop in Charleston, and I've been involved in the case less than twenty-four hours. We'll find the tea set."

"Do you really think a piece that important is going to turn up in a common place like a pawnshop?"

On top of every other complication in his life at the moment, did he really need a nun educating him about police procedure? "We have to pursue every possibility."

"While you're pursuing, Deputy, please make sure the history of the island is considered. How can we move forward if we don't know our past?"

"I'll adopt that as my campaign slogan." When she continued to stare at him, saying nothing, he sighed. She wouldn't be passed off with vague promises and a pat on the head. He'd been delusional to even believe in the prospect.

He, like most islanders, suspected her habit was steel-lined.

"So, Mrs. Jackson's claim about the set once belonging to the president is true?" he asked.

The sister nodded. "The historical society verified her genealogy years ago. Though she isn't a direct descendant of his as she often claims. President Jackson actually fathered no children. She's the great-great-granddaughter of his wife's brother."

"So how does she have the name Jackson?"

"A coincidence, believe it or not. Though I'm sure she'd tell you it was fate or some such. I expect her pride in her name is one of the reasons she never married."

Well, that and the plentiful supply of hunky lifeguards to keep her entertained.

"Still, the tea set did belong to the president," the nun continued. "So, as I said earlier, I doubt we're going to find it in a pawnshop."

"We?"

"With the sheriff out of town, it falls to me to supervise this case."

Knowing it would be rude and disrespectful to ask *how the hell do you figure that?* Tyler merely raised his eyebrows. "It does, huh?"

"Yes, it does. I represent the island's interests, the historical society and the church. Surely you feel you can trust me with the information on the case."

"Of course I trust you, Sister." In his meddling hometown, was there any way he really thought he could be in charge of a simple burglary without interference? He'd led covert international flight missions with less interrogation.

He forced a smile. "I'd be grateful for any insight you could give me into the case."

She leaned forward and laid her pale, vein-covered hand over his. "You'll make a good sheriff, Tyler."

Suddenly, he felt the weight of his own history, the fear of the future. His family expected a great deal from him, and for the first time in his life he wasn't sure he could measure up. After his last, disastrous mission, his confidence had taken a huge blow. Would he ever recover completely?

"I certainly hope to be," he said.

"So…the pawnshops."

Shifting his thoughts to the theft and its motives, he leaned back in his chair. "Have you considered the idea that the thief doesn't know the silver's historical significance?"

"No," she said, looking impressed. "I haven't."

"An employee who's desperate for money could have lifted the set without forcing the lock."

"Simon Iverson is her great-nephew. He doesn't have financial problems, but he's in her house frequently. He knows everyone who works there."

As Tyler wrote the name on his pad, he also made a note to check those financial records. Just in case.

"And the church occasionally brings meals to Henrietta. She actually sponsors our home missions project."

"Which means?"

"She bought our van, and her annual donation pays for nearly our entire budget of supplies to make meals that volunteers take to those who're sick or housebound and can't come to church. Her only stipulation is that she be included in the deliveries once a week. She's lonely and likes to be catered to."

Tyler really didn't want to fulfill the lonely needs of Mrs. Henrietta Jackson, but that didn't negate his duty to see her case through. "I'll need the names of the volunteers who delivered the meals."

"I'll check my records and let you know." She smiled, then added, "I'm glad you've given this so much thought. Do you have a theory about who might have taken the set?"

"I'm not sure about a theory yet, but two things stand out to me—the stealth of the theft, and the difficulty of profiting from the act. If the thief was smart enough not to get caught taking the silver and also understood its value, then he or she had to know reselling it would be complicated."

"A smart criminal and a dumb crime."

Now it was Tyler's turn to be impressed. "You're very skilled at succinctness, Sister."

"It helps when teaching Proverbs to teenagers."

"You also seem to know quite a bit about police procedure."

She waved her hand. "Reruns of TV cop shows. Perhaps the thief is a professional."

"Then why take only the tea set? She keeps enough jewelry in her bedroom to open her own museum. Plus there was a safe, which was not-so-cleverly hidden behind a painting in the library. It hadn't been touched."

"The silver could be valuable to a collector. What if a thief was hired to get that one thing?"

"That's possible, but how would I find a collector who—" He ground to a halt as an idea occurred to him. An idea about who might know about collectors who would obtain a coveted piece and not ask too many questions about how it had been acquired.

"Tyler?" Sister Mary Katherine prompted.

"Yes, ma'am?"

"You have a theory?"

"Just a possible source on finding an unscrupulous collector."

"Excellent. I'll let you get started."

As she rose, Tyler stood as well. "Sister, one last thing…" He rounded the desk and took her arm to escort her out. "We also have to consider the possibility that the silver set hasn't been stolen at all. Just…misplaced."

Her face flushed, she nodded. "Yes, I guess we do."

"It would also be helpful if the victim wasn't intent on blaming aliens for her property loss."

"Henrietta has a vivid imagination."

"There was mention of zipping and bopping—whatever those are."

"I'll try to counsel her—and hopefully get a straight answer. I wouldn't want the set to turn up at a jeweler's, where she'd sent it to be cleaned, leaving you only with an embarrassing story in the newspaper."

"The newspaper?" Tyler echoed absently, his mind already on finding a persuasive way to get Andrea to help him.

"You know how Henrietta loves attention. She probably called them before you."

"I guess so."

She squeezed his arm. "Don't worry. The timing's perfect for you to get some good publicity for your campaign."

Frankly, Tyler wasn't worried about the paper. Or the case.

He was worried about Andrea.

She was obviously attracted to him. Why wouldn't she go out with him? Maybe he'd simply been too presumptive earlier, asking her out on such short notice. Maybe dinner was too much. A drink was more casual. Not so significant.

After walking the sister to her car, he returned to the office—where Aqua was now reading about the latest trends in platform sandals—and went in search of Dwayne.

He found his fellow deputy in the records room. Dwayne liked alphabetizing things.

Watching him doggedly plow through a metal filing cabinet, humming under his breath, Tyler remembered that he and Dwayne shared something besides a job title. Trouble with a woman.

Everybody on the island knew Dwayne was completely in love with Misty Mickerson, a teller at the local bank. He'd been asking her out, like clockwork, every two weeks since her divorce two years ago. It was common knowledge that the only thing positive Misty's ex had given her was her three-year-old son. The rest had been dark and abusive.

Romantics believed Misty would eventually heal and accept Dwayne's offer. Cynics thought he was tilting at windmills.

Tyler finally understood his fellow deputy's sentiment and determination.

"Hey, Dwayne, what do you know about Simon Iverson?"

"Mrs. Jackson's nephew? He lives off Third Avenue. I think he's an engineer at a firm in Charleston."

"A nice house?"

"Sure."

"But not beachside." As fine a reason as any to resent a wealthy relative. "Does he have a good relationship with his aunt?"

"As far as I know."

"Can you call around and try to find out for sure?"

"Yes, s—" He stopped, his cheeks reddened.

He had the feeling he was fighting a losing battle about the *sir* thing. "How about calling me *lieutenant?*" he suggested. "That's at least a rank I've earned."

Dwayne's face immediately brightened. "Absolutely, Lieutenant. And I'll get on the nephew angle right after I get this drawer straightened out."

"Good. I'm headed out to the pool boy's place. We can compare notes later."

"You sure you don't need me as backup?"

Even if he had, Tyler wouldn't have said so and scared the life out of Dwayne. Exposure to Mrs. Jackson had been enough excitement for one day. "If he swings his surfboard at me, I'll duck."

Tyler headed to the front room to put the other half of his crack team to work. "Aqua, I need a background check on Simon Iverson. His address should be somewhere on Third."

Without looking up from her magazine, she muttered, "Dweeb."

Surely she meant Iverson. Tyler didn't think he'd lost his charm that significantly. "You don't like him?"

"He's okay. Just dweebie. I'm on it, boss."

Risking a brief glance at the magazine to note the engrossing pictorial debate on London Sheraton's latest toe polish color, he reluctantly nodded. "I can see that."

5

IT WAS MONDAY EVENING and Andrea fought the urge to look around the bar. Again.

Instead, she sipped her chardonnay and stared at the rippling waves crashing onto the sandy shore. The increase in tourism over the summer had prompted a local fisherman to open his own restaurant/bar on the beach, bringing the number of restaurants on the island up to a grand total of six.

Since it was mere blocks from her house, Andrea had eaten at Coconut Joe's quite a few times over the last several months. The building hovered on planks above the sand a bare hundred yards from the Atlantic. The decor was casual beach shack circa 1950—surfboards and framed shells on the walls, fishing nets draped from the high, wooden-plank ceiling, mismatched wicker chairs and bar-stools and tabletops that were lacquered board game classics like Monopoly and Scrabble.

The food, however, was first-class.

"Don't tell me you're being stood up," Sammy the bartender—and Joe's oldest son—asked with raised eyebrows.

"I don't think so. I'm just early." She didn't want to bring up the humiliating fact that she'd needed a drink to prepare for her drink.

"Hello there, Sammy," a familiar voice said from behind her, and she turned to have the pleasure of watching darkly handsome Carr Hamilton slide onto the barstool next to her. "And Andrea, of course. Now that I've made the world safe for litigation, I deserve a drink."

"Should that be safe *from* litigation?" she asked.

"Definitely not. It's every American's right to make their fortune from adversity."

"As long as you get thirty percent."

"Exactly." Smiling, he sipped his drink, a smooth Canadian whiskey she knew from experience. "Drinking alone, are we?"

"She has a date," Sammy offered.

Carr's dark brown eyes twinkled. "Does she now?"

"With the sheriff," Sammy added.

"The future sheriff—possibly," Andrea corrected. "And it's not a date. It's business."

"You might not want to tell people you have business with the sheriff," Sammy said. "Most of his business associates are behind bars." He headed off to fill another customer's order.

"Handy then that your lawyer is here." Carr grinned. "You and Tyler Landry, huh?"

Thankfully, Carr was five years older than her and didn't know about her embarrassing crush back in high school. He just liked to tease her about her love life. Or lack thereof.

Why couldn't she fall for brilliant, steady and gorgeous Carr? They were both native islanders, practically neighbors—Carr owned a stunning modern house on the point. When she'd started coming home more often to see her brother, they had actually gone out a few times, but somehow the sparks never flew. They'd become good friends instead, and as an attorney Carr had even recommended a colleague who specialized in troubled teens to defend her brother. His gang involvement had led him to a career in stealing cars, landing him a five-year sentence in prison. With the attorney's help, he'd gotten Finn counseling and an early parole.

"It has to do with a case of his," she said to Carr.

"Mrs. Jackson's silver tea service."

Andrea nearly choked on her wine. She didn't imagine Tyler wanted his business spread around like gossip among the islanders. One of these folks was a thief, after all. "How'd you know that?"

He ticked off the facts on his fingers. "Stolen historical item. Pushy owner who wants answers. And you with all your degrees in useless ancient history and stuff." He sipped his whiskey. "I got an *A* in deductive reasoning at Yale."

"It's the *and stuff* that made me a cinch for the job."

"Not to mention you have much better legs than Deputy Dwayne."

"No kidding, this is strictly business. I'm going to do what I can to help him with the case, and that's it. I mean, me and The Great Tyler Landry? Who'd buy that relationship? He's a war hero, for heaven's sake. A couple of years ago, when I was living in Washington, the *Post* did a special story on him, about him saving an entire country or something."

"I think it was a village, actually."

"Right. He got some super-duper-special medal."

"The Congressional Medal of Honor."

She gestured with her wineglass. "That's the one. So,

me and him? That's—" It suddenly occurred to her that she was both rambling and not telling her friend anything he wasn't already aware of. "How do you know all this?"

"The wires picked up his story. The *Island Gazette* dedicated the entire paper to him. Plus, he's running for sheriff of my island, and I'm an informed citizen. But I still don't see what medals he does or doesn't own have to do with you two seeing each other."

"Trust me, it does."

"Andrea?"

Whirling, she faced Tyler and prayed he hadn't overheard her and Carr's conversation. "Hey."

He'd taken the time to change from his deputy's uniform and wore jeans and a pale yellow polo shirt that stretched across his broad chest and accented his tan skin. She barely resisted the urge to hum in appreciation.

His gaze went from her to her half-empty glass and then to Carr. "We said seven-thirty, right?"

"We did. I just got here early." After she made the introductions between the two men, she added, "Carr lives down the beach from me."

"Really?"

Noting Tyler's cool tone, she wondered if he was in a hurry or if he was bothered by finding her with another man. He'd made it clear on the phone that this wasn't a date; it was a business meeting. Still, she had to admit she'd be less than excited if she arrived to find him sharing a drink with another woman.

They had a seriously screwed-up relationship.

Sammy approached at that moment to take Tyler's drink order. "I think we're going to move down," she said, pointing to the end of the row of barstools. "See ya, Carr."

As she scooped up her wine, Carr asked quietly, "Are you sure you don't want me to come with you and make sure your civil rights aren't violated?"

"I'm perfectly safe."

He glanced over her head at Tyler, then back at her. "Don't be too sure about that."

Ignoring that loaded comment, she hitched her purse on her shoulder, then headed off to her new seat, hoping Tyler would follow.

He did, saying nothing until Sammy set a bottle of beer in front of him. "Was he your dinner date last night?"

"Carr? No."

"Are you sleeping with him?"

What the hell? "That's—"

Tyler held up his hand to stop her. "Sorry. None of my business." He took a sip of beer. "It's been a really frustrating day."

"I can tell. Why don't we—"

"Well, Patsy, if it isn't our future sheriff and our favorite art historian." Betsy Johnson, along with her constant sidekick, Patsy Smith, approached Andrea and Tyler.

Patsy frowned. "How many art historians do we actually know, Betsy?"

"Well, only one," Betsy admitted. "But she is very smart and talented."

Patsy sighed. "Alone, though."

"True, but so is the future sheriff, as we learned last night."

"Is he really the only sheriff we know?" Patsy asked, angling her head.

"Unless your nephew—"

"Ladies," Andrea interrupted, knowing the pattern of

banter and matchmaking well from her childhood, "do you want to have this conversation all by yourselves, or did you need us for a reason?"

Betsy's lips pursed in irritation as Patsy spoke. "We actually came to Joe's for a grouper sandwich. He makes the best on the island, you know."

Andrea glanced at Tyler, who'd at least lost his glum expression. "I know."

Betsy nodded. "But we saw Tyler and had to come over and remind him that Wednesday night is the Dolphin Club meeting."

"The what?" Tyler asked.

"It's like the Rotary Club," Patsy explained, "but we islanders like to be a bit more unique."

Betsy nodded. "They raise money to build homes for impoverished children in foreign countries mostly, but with the election so close at hand…"

"Two weeks from tomorrow," Patsy said.

Andrea could see where this was leading. "You thought Tyler could speak at the meeting and get the support of the Dolphins."

"They're very influential," Betsy said.

Patsy smiled. "Sheriff Caldwell's a member."

"I'll be there," Tyler said quickly, clearly catching the hint. "Thank you for inviting me."

"You, too, Andrea." Patsy patted her hand. "It's such a lovely social occasion. The Dolphins have a private club on Sixth Avenue where the party will take place."

"And we're providing the food," Betsy said proudly, waving as she and Patsy turned away. "Don't be late."

"The campaign rolls on," Andrea said, meeting Tyler's gaze and noting his slumped posture.

"As well as the case."

"How about dinner?" She grinned. "I hear Joe makes a great grouper sandwich."

He returned her smile, but weakly. "Sure."

She called Sammy over and ordered the sandwiches, after which she reflected on Tyler's uncharacteristic slumped posture. Had running into Carr really bothered him so much or was it simply the case frustrating him?

She was pretty sure she could eliminate worry about the Dolphins party. "No leads on the silver?" she asked.

"None. I talked to her pool maintenance guy today, but he says he never even goes in the house."

"Except when Mrs. Jackson tries to lure him inside with a nice, cold glass of lemonade?"

He glanced at her, and his lips tipped up. "Pretty much."

"Kirk is definite luring material, so you can't blame the old gal for trying."

The frown returned. "Is he really? I guess he maintains your pool, too."

"He does. He also isn't bright enough to have pulled off stealing a ham sandwich out of the fridge, much less a priceless silver set from a locked cabinet."

"No, he's not." The scowl lines in Tyler's forehead deepened. "How did you know the tea set was in a locked cabinet?"

"I've seen it. Has anybody told you that you have a very expressive face?"

He focused that laser beam blue gaze on her, compelling her heart to kick up its rhythm. "Never."

"Maybe I'm just perceptive." Especially when it came to him. She'd spent many high school lunch hours hiding behind a book she was pretending to read while really watching every smile, laugh and frown that crossed his face as he sat at the next table over.

Shaking away the uncomfortable memory, she said, "You're luring material, too. I'll bet Mrs. Jackson is thrilled to have you on the case instead of Sheriff Caldwell. Maybe she stole the set herself to get you over there."

He leaned toward her. "You think?"

As always, his attention made her feel self-conscious. She fought for a light tone. "Maybe." She grinned, then added, "Personally, I found the disguise route works wonders."

"And you chose to put your devious plan into motion for me instead of Kirk." He paused significantly. "Or Carr Hamilton."

"I did."

"Why?"

"I already told you why."

"I'm your fantasy."

"You were."

"But not anymore?"

She swallowed. How had they traveled down this road again? His smile, his body and his wit added layers and layers of heat to an attraction that was already a blazing bonfire. The idea of touching him again was beyond tempting; it was a fever she worried she'd suffer from forever.

"Andrea?" he prompted in a low voice that made her tingle from head to toe.

As a stall tactic—and not an incredibly clever one—she sipped her wine. "I thought we were here for a business meeting."

"We are. Does that mean all other subjects are off-limits?"

"No, but can we talk about the case first?"

He shrugged, opening the folder on the bar in front of

him, then sliding it over. "You were the one who brought up disguises."

"So I was." With more reluctance than she wished she felt, she broke her gaze from his and focused on the pictures of the tea set. "The detail and variety of angles on the shots are nice. I never got a close-up look in person."

"Mrs. Jackson's insurance agent is very efficient."

"Could you e-mail me copies, too? They'll be helpful when I'm contacting colleagues."

"No problem."

"You certainly need to get it back. It's a lovely representation of Revere's work."

"Revere?" He made a choking sound, causing her to look at him. "You mean as in *Paul* Revere?"

"Yes. See here?" She pointed at a picture of the back of a teaspoon, the initials PR in italic lettering and appearing slightly raised. "I'll have to do a bit more research, but we can generally narrow down the time frame to the late 1700s."

"*The British are coming, the British are coming.* That dude made this?"

"Yes, though that's not exactly what he said. Still—"

"No wonder everybody's losing their mind over a bit of silver."

Having regular contact with insurance executives who cared much more for the bottom line than the beauty of the pieces they represented, she smiled. "I expect somebody from the island historical society will be bending your ear about this case very soon."

"Sister Mary Katherine came by already."

"She's not one for hanging in the background. Do you have any leads?"

"I checked out Mrs. Jackson's nephew."

"Simon?"

"You know him?"

Dweeb, she thought. But since she'd been called the same thing many times, she didn't voice this word. "In passing."

"He certainly had the opportunity to take it, but he claims they have a good relationship, and he has a stable job and a good credit rating. I need to do some more digging to be sure."

He sighed, and Andrea wished she felt comfortable offering him a hug. This whole plan to have her fantasy and move on was failing miserably.

"So besides considering Mrs. Jackson stashed the thing under the bed just for the sake of drama," he continued, "I've checked with pawnshops all over the area. But knowing about the Revere angle makes that even less likely than I originally thought."

"Which is what led you to me."

"Right."

Sammy brought the sandwiches, which Tyler pronounced excellent, sending the bartender back to his other customers with a proud smile.

Tyler sipped his beer. "If we're working with the angle that the thief knew the value and significance of what he was taking, then he likely either wanted it for himself or he has a discrete buyer already lined up."

"That would make the most sense. I know collectors out there who might want something and not ask too many questions about where it came from."

Surprise flashed in his eyes. "Collectors you know personally?"

"We're not best buddies or anything, but yes. I even know a couple of thieves."

"They actually make a living stealing things?"

"Not anymore. And not ever on paper, if you know what I mean. But when something's missing, they're the first people I call."

"Next time try calling the cops."

"No way. These guys are valuable sources." When he opened his mouth to argue, she shook her head. "One of them actually spent some time in prison, but neither has done anything illegal I know about."

"Lately."

She hid her smile by sipping her wine. "Lately," she confirmed after a pause. "Regardless of how I know them, the important thing for you is that I can ask around about the tea set in places you don't have access to."

"Make sure you tell your sources you're sleeping with a cop."

"I doubt they'd be interested in my one-night stand."

Clearly irritated, he shoved his empty plate to the side. "Is there a particular reason you're determined to diminish our relationship?"

"We don't have a—" She stopped at the fiery burst of anger in his eyes. "We can't make anything from a night of lies," she said quietly, even reasonably, considering he seemed determined to cover the same ground over and over.

"I don't see why not. I'd rather you were honest with me from here on out, but the way we started shouldn't matter." His gaze searched hers. "In fact, I think we started out pretty great. Have dinner with me."

"I just did."

He inched closer, so one of his legs slid intimately between hers, then laid his arm across the back of her stool. "On purpose this time, not using work as an excuse."

Her heart started its familiar racing whenever he was close. "I think that's a really bad idea."

"Why? What—" He stopped, staring at her. "Wait a second. There *is* a particular reason. It's not that you don't want me. You want me too much."

Not liking the realization that he was way too close to the truth, she tried to be annoyed. "That's some ego you've got there, Deputy."

"So you don't want me."

She couldn't look into his eyes and continue to pretend she didn't want him more than she wanted to breathe, so she stared at the floor. Protecting her heart from him was an instinct she'd been giving in to for so long, she didn't know how to be any other way. "It won't work between us."

"Dammit, Andrea."

Startled, she lifted her head.

He rose, tossing some bills on the bar. "Call me if you get any leads on the case."

Then he turned and walked away, shoving open the bar's patio door and stalking across the dimly lit back deck and disappearing down the stairs to the beach.

TYLER CONSIDERED HIMSELF stubborn, but he'd never been the type to bang his head against a wall.

But then he couldn't ever remember being this frustrated in his entire life.

Frankly, most things came to him pretty easily. He was naturally athletic, so sports and the physical challenges of the military had been met with focus and determination. He was popular with women and had plenty of friends of both sexes. His intelligence was sufficient to do his job, and he was a good problem solver. Even the high school math Andrea had tutored him in hadn't been caused by lack of understanding so much as time management with all the other things going on in his life.

Until a few months ago his life was near perfect.

Until he'd made a poor decision and cost three men their lives.

So was he going to walk away from this challenge? Away from her the way he'd retired from his job? Was he going to accept another failure?

Could he?

With the glowing moon overhead and a few floodlights from houses as his only guide, he continued aimlessly strolling through the sand. Was he being cosmically or divinely punished for the mistakes he'd made during his last mission?

He couldn't feel more pain and regret or do more than give up the goals and leadership that had been the driving force all his adult life. Much as he'd like to, he couldn't rewrite the past.

When he sensed someone walking behind him, he turned without much curiosity. He wasn't in the mood to talk to anybody.

He stopped and nearly stumbled when he saw Andrea, walking barefoot and briskly in his shadow, carrying her shoes, her bright pink sundress flapping in the breeze.

"Would it really bother you if I was sleeping with Carr?" she asked the moment she reached him.

Frustrating, confusing and completely unpredictable—that was Andrea Hastings. Not knowing where this was going, but seeing no reason not to be honest, he nodded. "Hell, yes."

"Why?"

"I'm not sharing."

"Me in particular or anybody?"

He had no idea where this conversation was going, but he sensed if he gave the wrong answer, she'd turn around and march back the way she'd come.

Since he had no idea what answer she wanted, he figured the only thing he had was the truth. Hadn't she told him about her teenage fantasy and the reason she'd kept her identity a secret?

"I've been in exclusive relationships before, but not in years. My work has been my biggest priority. Women are…" He shrugged as he trailed off. It seemed callous to be so indifferent about his love life.

"Just there?" she finished for him.

"Yeah." He shoved his hands in the back pockets of his jeans. "They were. Until I met you."

"What's different about me?"

"You're everywhere." When she stood silent, watching him, he realized that hadn't made any sense at all, though his reasoning seemed clear to him. Stepping close to her and wishing he could touch her without being rejected, he drew a deep breath. "I can't stop thinking about you. My interest in my job, finding the silver set, even the election keeps waning. I swear I smell your perfume when I'm in the office and nothing's really there except the ancient scent of coffee and doughnuts. Every time I see the color green, I compare it to the shade of your eyes. I barely slept last night wondering what you were doing, who you were having dinner with. When I walked in tonight and saw you sitting next to another guy, I wanted to punch him and—"

She tossed her shoes in the sand, threw her arms around his neck and kissed him.

Apparently, he'd given the right answer.

He held her against his chest, angling his head to deepen the kiss, sliding his tongue against hers, reveling in the beating of her heart in rapid time with his.

He was already addicted to her touch, and the idea of her walking away from him was so painful to consider, he deliberately blocked out the memory of the despair he'd been feeling just moments ago.

"What does my perfume smell like?" she asked when she pulled back, breathing hard.

Ducking his head, he drew in the scent clinging to her skin just below her ear, even though he could have described it easily from memory. "Oranges, plus something sweet and fresh like herbs."

She smiled. "It's called Citrus Breeze."

He smoothed her windblown hair back from her face. "My senses have always been pretty acute."

"Also…" After picking up her shoes, she took his hand and led him farther down the beach, away from the bar and toward her house, which he realized must be only a couple of blocks away. "I'll help you find the silver. Carr and I are currently friends and have always been just friends. Last night I had dinner with Finn, my younger brother."

Relief flooded him. "Your brother."

"Yep. He's also an ex-thief, though not either of the ones I was talking about earlier. He was in a gang and convicted of grand theft auto. Six months ago, he was given early parole, which is why I moved home to work on a consulting basis and cut back on my travel."

"Your parents?" he asked, though he was pretty sure he

knew the answer. Why else would a sister feel solely responsible for her younger sibling?

"They died in a car accident two years ago."

"I'm sorry."

She squeezed his hand. "Thanks. It's been hard, but their sudden deaths brought about a big change in Finn. He was really haunted by the idea that they'd died thinking of him as a criminal. With Carr's help, I found an attorney who could help him work toward getting paroled."

"And part of that plan was you moving back to the island?"

"It was my idea. I traveled a lot of years without responsibility to anybody but myself. I couldn't do that anymore," she said, her tone a little wistful. "Mostly, I like being home again. I have friends and Sister Mary Katherine here to back me up. She gave Finn's job at the rectory, doing maintenance projects and running errands. And I love my house."

"I think you're pretty amazing to sacrifice so much for your brother."

"You'd do the same for your sisters."

His head whipped toward her. "How did you know I have sisters?"

"Teresa and Tammy, six and three years older than you respectively," she said proudly. "Your mom's name is Sophia and your father's is John, which is also your middle name. They live at 403 East 8th Avenue. Oh, and your grandfather was Sheriff Austin Landry, who served back in the day before Sloan's dad." Obviously noticing the shocked expression on his face, she added, "I used to study you with much more intensity than everybody thought I did math."

He wasn't sure how to reply to that. An uncomfortable silence fell—at least on his part. "Okay, that's a little weird," he said finally.

"Yeah, I guess so." But she didn't seem bothered by it. "I already apologized for not noticing you then, didn't I?"

"You did." With a determined nod, she said, "It's fine. I've got to stop living in the past—no matter how much being home brings it all back."

"If I could change the past, I would."

They'd reached her house, and she stopped, turning to face him in a circle of illumination from a floodlight. The focus and devotion on her upturned face startled him. She was letting down the wall she'd put up between them.

"You would?" she asked softly.

"Sure."

Studying her beautiful features and wondering if he'd simply been blind or stupid at eighteen, he wrapped his arms around her waist. All day he'd been trying to pinpoint the exact shade of her eyes and now realized they reminded him of a trip once to Figi. The ocean there was pure and clear and, in shallow water, the exact same pale green.

Not long after those brief, idyllic days, he'd been called to the mission that had ended his career. And lives.

Maybe you don't deserve her.

Panic washed over him for a crazy moment before he suppressed the emotion. She didn't have to know what he'd done.

"I think you're pretty amazing," he said, cupping her cheek in his hand.

Her gaze, a pool of liquid green he wanted to drown in, held his before she spoke. "That's beginning to sink in. By the way," she added, angling her face so her mouth was near his. "I'd love to have dinner with you sometime."

"It's a little late for dinner."

"How about dessert?"

6

SINCE HE'D STARTED the day with a nun in his office giving him theoretical hell about solving a case of missing historic silver, and he was ending it by sitting in a hot tub with a bikini-clad blonde he was nuts about, Tyler considered his near-perfect life firmly back on track.

"Comfy?" Andrea asked, sitting several feet away but occasionally tangling her legs with his under the water.

He adjusted his boxers, which were substituting for his swimsuit. "How likely is it your brother'll drop by tonight?"

"He has a strict curfew and his own apartment on church grounds. I wouldn't say there's a zero chance, but I work in insurance, so I never do."

"I like absolutes. Part of that pesky military training." Narrowing his eyes, he scooted closer to her. "Where is he?"

"Why?"

"I'd like to actually meet him before he finds me seducing his sister in the hot tub."

"He's helping the nuns set up a youth sleepover at the church."

"Sleepover? I don't recall any sleepovers."

"They don't really sleep. The kids hang out and play video games and volleyball in the gym all night. The

Sisters supervise. It's all fun and innocent. Strawberry?" she asked, holding a plate of fruit between them.

Even with only the accent lighting shining up the stalks of the palm trees and the ethereal, bubbling blue of the water, he could easily see the laughter on her face. Her humor was just one of the many reasons she was irresistible.

After taking a strawberry, he set the plate on the deck beside them. He took a bite of the fruit, then offered the other half to her.

When she opened her mouth, he replaced the strawberry with his lips. She sighed against him, laying her palm on his bare chest. He indulged in the sweet taste of her tongue, striving to calm the anxiety he could feel vibrating through her body.

"Are you nervous about being alone with me?" he whispered against her lips.

She shook her head. "We've been alone before."

"Not like this." He trailed his mouth across her cheek, relishing the smoothness of her skin, the citrus scent of her perfume that wrapped seductive tendrils around him and drew him further under her spell. "This is different. You and me, knowing who we are. What we want."

She licked her lips, her gaze dropping to his. "And what do you want?"

"You." He inched closer, until their bare thighs brushed. "Not just your body this time, but your mind and heart. I want to hear you say my name. I want nothing between us."

"But, how—"

He silenced her question with another kiss. He appreciated her keen mind, her drive and desire to solve the puzzles in her life, even if one of those puzzles involved him and queries he wasn't ready to face.

Tonight he wanted steam and heat and…her. Just her.

It seemed he'd been waiting for her all his life. Some part of him had sparked with a need to claim, to take and possess as soon as he'd seen her walking by him like a ghost from the past in frothy, pure sky-blue.

"Tyler," she whispered, and his heart raced.

Then it jumped when she wrapped her arms around his neck and pressed her chest against his.

His body hardened at her touch. His blood heated, and he tugged her through the bubbling water and into his lap, her legs straddling his hips. Wrapping his hands around her waist, he pressed against her lower back, and groaned as his erection found the answering pulse between her thighs.

Slick skin, needy touches, greedy senses.

The sensations melded together in the steam as he untied her bikini, and she helped him remove his boxers. They slid against each other, his hand diving between her legs, eliciting the moan of his name he'd been longing for. Her hand wrapped around his erection, sliding up then down with brisk assurance.

"Dear…" she gasped suddenly.

He trailed his mouth up her jaw, feeling her climactic pulse around his fingers.

"…Tyler," she added, shuddering.

"There's more," he assured her.

Flopped against his body, she panted. "Not sure I can take it."

"Sure you can."

He swung her up and out of the water, adrenaline and need giving him much-needed strength. Earlier, while she'd been fussing with her strawberry dessert, he'd been busy placing condoms within easy reach of the hot tub. He grabbed one of the packages now, and tore into the foil with his teeth.

Protection in place and sitting on the side of the tub, the lower half of his legs dangling in the water, he moved her over him and onto his pulsing erection, closing his eyes at the intense pleasure that surged through him as she took him into her body.

Caught up in the sensation herself or just mercifully realizing he craved immediate movement, she rocked against his hips.

Pleasure shot down his spine.

He clung to her, absorbing the silky wetness of her skin, tight fit of her femininity surrounding him, the sea breeze rushing over them.

When everything inside him tightened in anticipation of orgasm, he pressed her hips closer, hoping she'd climax again, with him, giving them both the bond their bodies craved and their souls longed for.

With a jerk, she gripped his shoulders, and he knew they were as one. He closed his eyes. His lips found the base of her throat at the exact place her pulse raced. He lost control of the pleasure soaring through every cell of his body.

They were together.

Not before, and maybe not even after. But, for now, he was everything to her, and her to him.

It was more than he'd hoped for.

Probably more than he deserved.

SHE WORE HIS SHIRT and nothing else.

Even her mental defenses had vanished.

She was trying to regret running onto the beach after

Tyler and impulsively leading him back to her house, inviting him into her life and bed. But as she stood on the deck outside her bedroom, watching the moon slide in and out of the clouds, the shadows of the palms dancing across the sand, she acknowledged she felt better than she ever had in her life.

Sex with Tyler wasn't awkward groping or missed timing or lacking in emotion. It was special and real and… amazing. The mere memory of his touch made her heart beat faster.

Why couldn't she, for once, stop considering the future based on actuary tables or past predictors? Why couldn't she enjoy herself without worrying about the downside? Why couldn't she indulge in the attention of a man she'd considered her fantasy ideal for half her life?

She wanted to do all those things.

On the other hand, if she could take out an insurance policy on them, she'd do it in a blink.

When his arms encircled her from behind, she closed her eyes and leaned back into him.

"I thought you were asleep," she said.

"I was," he returned, his voice scratchy in an intimate way that made her heart flip over in her chest. "But I realized you weren't with me anymore."

"I come out here when I'm restless."

"You should be exhausted." He brushed her hair to the side, then pressed his lips to her nape. "But if you're not…"

"This is crazy. This can't work."

"You're so right," he said calmly, then kissed her just behind her ear. "It's going really lousy so far."

"I'm serious." She turned in his arms, intending to push him back. That brilliant plan would have worked if she hadn't gotten an eyeful of him, his broad, muscled, tanned chest bare and wearing nothing but his jeans, which he'd neglected to button all the way. Her mouth went dry. "I'm…"

Angling his head, he threaded his fingers through her hair. His blue-eyed gaze locked on her face, he lowered his head and kissed her—thoroughly, slowly, deeply.

"What were you saying?" he asked when he pulled back after what seemed like hours.

She wrapped her arms around his neck. "I have absolutely no idea."

LIKE A DÉJÀ VU NIGHTMARE, Tyler woke to his cell phone ringing.

Before answering, he reached out beside him in the bed. Finding Andrea's bare hip, he turned toward her, pulling her back against him. At least this morning-after wouldn't begin like the last one.

As he groped for his phone, he made a mental note to spend nights at her house from now on so she couldn't run out on him.

"This had better be good," he said into the phone without opening his eyes.

"Up and at 'em, Lieutenant." It was Aqua's voice. "I've got a problem here."

"If the rosebush vandal was in action last night, I'll handle it when I get in. Unless it's an emergency, Aqua, you really need to save your calls for a decent hour."

"How do you feel about nine-oh-five?"

Andrea turned, kissing his chest, her warm hands wandering downward, and Tyler vowed to become a pool boy before he'd put up with the sheriff business. "I'll be there before eight, so that sounds fine."

"Boss, you missed eight a while back."

"I—" With his senses clearing, he heard a commotion in the background on Aqua's end. He opened his eyes and found Andrea's bedroom dim—and her lips working their way across his jaw. He tugged her against his growing erection and considered hanging up on his dispatcher. "If this is some kind of test the sheriff put you up to, it's not funny. What time is it?"

"Nine-oh-six."

"No way."

But the sound in the background grew in volume, and Tyler felt his first fissure of true worry.

He craned his neck around to find the digital clock on Andrea's bedside table: *9:06.*

He sat straight up. "Damn."

"Tyler?" Andrea asked, her voice thick and groggy.

"What's going on, Aqua?" he asked into the phone.

"I want you to know I have confidence in your abilities, which is why I called you first instead of bugging the sheriff in the middle of his vacation."

"Really?" Somehow he didn't think it was confidence in his abilities, but the sheriff's wrath she considered. He wasn't due back until right before the election, which was still two weeks away. "What's wrong?"

"We have a situation. A sort of immediate one. Listen."

The background noise he'd heard before became two male voices, both raised in anger. He rolled out of bed and was on his feet in a second. "Are they armed?"

"Don't think so."

"Where's Dwayne?"

"Hiding in the records room."

"Shut your door and lock it."

"Already done."

"Stay on the line. I'll be right there." He jumped into his jeans, strapped on his ankle holster, found his shirt tossed on the dresser and his shoes... Hell, they were probably still outside. "I gotta go," he whispered to a confused Andrea, who'd sat up, wrapping the sheet around her body.

"Is it serious?" she asked, her eyes jumping to alert.

"Could be. I'll—" He stopped, knowing he didn't have time for pretty words. Leaning over, he kissed her, inhaled her scent and wished he could linger. "We can talk later, okay?"

"Sure. You want me to come with you?"

"No." He was already in a partial panic about Aqua. "I can—" His truck was back at Joe's. *Damn, damn, damn.* Some sheriff he'd make. "I need your car."

"My keys are on the kitchen counter downstairs."

"Thanks."

He kissed her one last time, then sped from the room and down the stairs.

Grateful, and not for the first time, he lived on a really small island, he was at the station in minutes, keeping the line open and talking to Aqua the entire time. The commotion was apparently caused by Roger Bampton and Cal Jones, rival team volleyball captains.

Since Tyler had only been back recently, he was unfamiliar with the intensity of adult volleyball competitions. He remembered his dad playing softball for St. Matthews—no shouting allowed. Sister Mary Katherine had her standards, after all.

"You know the Red Sox versus Yankees?" Aqua asked.

"Sure."

"Kittens rolling around on the floor with a ball of yarn compared to the annual June first Palmer's Island volleyball finals."

"This should be fun. I'll see you inside."

He disconnected the call as he leaped from Andrea's car. The police station was adjacent to city hall, but with its own entrance. Both buildings were historic, brick with stone steps. In the parking lot, he noticed two unfamiliar cars, one with the personalized plate CHAMP.

Yippee. Arguing egomaniac volleyball players.

When he slid inside, he was pleased to note both men stood practically nose to nose in the lobby and didn't even seem to be aware of Aqua's presence behind her glassed-in office.

However, they whipped their heads toward him as he let the front door bang shut behind him. "You two need to take a long step backward."

They stared at him for ten seconds, then resumed shouting.

"My trophy's missing, and he took it!" the tall, dark-haired, athletically thin guy yelled.

"It's not your trophy," the other guy—short, squatty with blond hair going on gray—returned in a disgusted tone. "You had so many ringers on your team you coulda gone professional."

"What a bunch of crap. Face it, Bampton. You lost." He laughed. "No surprise."

Bampton apparently had no intention of facing anything. His skin burned bright red. "Your setter played for team U.S.A. in the Olympics!"

Tall guy, who must be Cal, threw his hands up. "He bought a house on the beach. That's a crime now?"

Tyler crossed his arms over his chest while he watched

the exchange, and his thoughts returned to Andrea and the warm, cozy bed he'd left. He'd spent a lot of years serving his country, doing just that over and over. He'd grumbled over the lack of sleep and inconvenient timing, but he'd never resented his duty.

Until now.

He'd retired—early, somewhat reluctantly and under a cloud—to his quiet island home. Didn't he deserve some actual quiet?

Striding around the two idiot men, he approached the side door to Aqua's office, which she opened. "I need some cuffs."

After darting to a drawer, she laid the cool steel in his hand. "Where are yours?"

"In my truck."

She grinned knowingly. "Which is where—exactly?"

"Lock up," he said as he started to pull the door closed.

"That must have been some fish sandwich you had with Andrea Hastings."

Okay, maybe the island was a little *too* small.

Pushing personal issues aside, he shut the door, then turned, noting Roger and Cal were still shouting, completely unaware of their surroundings. And for the first time since he'd left active duty, he pulled his gun for something other than cleaning it.

He approached the men, holding his pistol in one hand and the handcuffs in the other. "At the moment, you've still got a choice," he said quietly.

Even amid the shouting, they obviously heard the determined tone. Blessed silence ensued.

They also got their asses hauled into cells. Separate ones. Which unfortunately got them shouting again.

After Tyler retrieved his fellow deputy from his records

room barricade, he called Andrea to tell her everything was fine and he'd have her car back within the hour. He gave Aqua a high five, then poured himself a fresh cup of coffee before wandering back down the hall to the cells.

Leaning against the wall, he sipped from his mug and eyed the sullen, now quiet, detainees. "You guys want to tell me what's going on?"

When they both starting shouting at once, he turned and headed back down the hall. He checked his e-mail while indulging in a daydream where the sheriff pinned his new badge to his chest after the election, while his family and Andrea clapped beside him.

An adoring look and kiss from Andrea followed. The perfect day.

After a bit, he headed down to the cells again. "You guys want to try again?"

"You can't keep us locked up in here," Roger said.

"I want my lawyer," Cal added.

Tyler nodded. "Sure. Where is he exactly? Charleston?" He deliberately glanced at his watch. "With spring break traffic and road construction delays, it shouldn't take him more than forty-five minutes to drive over. In the meantime, I can come up with some official charges. Disturbing the peace, terrorizing police officials—"

"You've lost your mind," Cal said, wrapping his hands around the bars. "I did no such thing."

"My fellow deputy and dispatcher were forced to barricade themselves out of harm's way in fear for their lives." Smiling, Tyler started out. "I'll get you a phone."

"Don't go!" Roger begged. "I'm the victim here. This idiot stormed into my house and accused me of taking his stupid trophy."

"You did," Cal insisted. "Who else would take it?"

"How should I know? Or even care?"

"When did you notice the trophy was missing?" Tyler asked, hoping to head off yet another screaming match.

"This morning. I got up to start the coffeepot and noticed the trophy was gone."

"Could it have been gone for a while?"

"No." His face reddened. "I polish it…frequently."

"Every frickin' morning probably," Roger said dryly.

Tyler silenced him with a glare. "Was the trophy kept in plain sight?" he asked Cal.

"On the mantel over the fireplace."

"Any sign of a break-in?"

"The back door was unlocked, but my mother sometimes leaves it open by accident."

"Your mother?"

"She doesn't get around too well, so I've been living with her since my divorce."

"Bad divorce?"

Cal shrugged. "No worse than most. And why would my ex want my trophy? It's silver but it probably has very little actual precious metal in it. It's the pride in having won."

The tips of Tyler's fingers tingled. "Silver, huh? You have a picture of it?"

"Sure." Cal reached into his back pocket for his cell phone, then flipped it open. A picture of him and his team hoisting the trophy was the background on his home screen. "I have some close-ups, too," he said, pushing the phone between the bars and into Tyler's hand.

And he certainly did. The cop was glad to have the details; the man was sincerely embarrassed for the guy.

"Who has access to the house besides you and your mother?"

"The cleaning service. Oh, and the church brings lunch to Mother a couple times a week. Both have keys in case she's not home."

And that was one coincidence too many. The tingle in his fingers became a full-fledged vibration. But how could the two cases be related? The volleyball trophy was silver—in color. It was worthless. The tea set was priceless.

"Do you know who brought lunch recently?" he asked, thinking of Sister Mary Katherine's list, which he'd yet to look over.

Cal shrugged. "She didn't say. I don't think it's any one person."

"I'll send Dwayne out to your mother's house within the hour." Tyler unlocked Cal's cell, then handed him a business card. "In the meantime, I'd appreciate you e-mailing me the pictures of the trophy."

"Yeah, sure."

Tyler unlocked Roger's cell as well. "In the future, gentlemen, call the office when you have a situation that requires our assistance instead of taking action on your own."

Roger nodded at Tyler, sent Cal a glare, then stormed off down the hall.

"He's a sore loser," Cal commented.

Tyler had been thinking Cal could be a better winner. As he escorted the latest "victim" back to the lobby, Tyler got Cal's mother's name and phone number. He needed to find out who had brought her lunch ASAP.

On his way to the sheriff's office, he stopped by the records room and gave Dwayne his assignment. "Be sure to dust the back door and mantel for fingerprints," he added.

Since, next to filing, that was Dwayne's favorite thing in the world to do, his coworker was smiling when Tyler left, the morning's trauma apparently forgotten.

Tyler called Mrs. Wells, wondering if this whole mess could be solved so quickly and easily. The tie between the delivered meals and the break-ins couldn't be ignored, yet he couldn't imagine anybody working for Sister Mary Katherine who wasn't completely honest.

In answer to his question about the identity of the last delivery person to Cal's place, Mrs. Wells said, "Oh, yes, I remember him. Such a nice boy."

"Who?"

"Finn Hastings."

It couldn't be. Andrea had said her brother did some work for the church, but...

Andrea's ex-con brother.

"Thank you, Mrs. Wells," he said in a hollow voice. "Deputy Burris will be by soon."

Hanging up, then dropping his forehead in his hands, he stared at the desk, the one that was supposed to be his in a matter of weeks. Provided he could keep everything under control in the sheriff's absence. Provided he could get back the missing silver pieces.

With dread firmly planted in his stomach, he searched his e-mail for the message from Sister Mary Katherine. Unfortunately, he found it. He read through the list of people who'd brought meals to Mrs. Jackson and saw a name and date that sent a chill down his spine.

Three days before her silver tea set went missing, Finn Hastings had brought her lunch.

7

"THIS IS GETTING TO be a regular thing," Andrea teased, stepping back to invite Tyler into her house.

No answering smile. No hug, kiss or any sign of the affectionate, I-can't-stop-touching-you man she'd spent the night with.

"We need to talk," he said simply.

She stood in front of him, noting he'd taken the time to shower and change clothes in the last few hours. His hair appeared damp, and he wore a freshly pressed khaki uniform, complete with pistol and holster. The metal on his badge caught the overhead light and flashed, as if in warning.

"Is there a reason you suddenly look like a cop?" Though her stomach felt hollow, she raised her eyebrows. "And not just because of the uniform."

"Yes." His eyes were bleak. "There's been another theft."

"Of what?"

"The island beach volleyball trophy."

She started to laugh, but one look into Tyler's remote gaze had her silencing the impulse abruptly.

"We should probably sit down," he said, his voice firm and expressionless.

Since this didn't seem like the kind of conversation for the cozy den or sun-brightened deck, she led him into the kitchen. She indicated one of the barstools that were tucked beneath the granite-topped bar in the center of the room.

"You want coffee or iced tea?"

"No, thank you." As she slid onto a stool, he lowered himself to one next to her. He laid her car keys on the counter between them. "Thanks for helping me out this morning."

Her throat tightened as she glanced briefly at them. Something was very, very wrong. She met his gaze and saw nothing of the confident, hunky hero she'd crushed on for so long.

This tension and uncertainty was ridiculous, she suddenly decided.

Hadn't she stopped being so cautious? Whatever the reason Tyler had come, he was in pain about it.

And old habits were hard to break.

Rising, she cupped his face between her hands. Before he could do more than widen his eyes, she kissed him. She angled her head and let the force of their passion flow through her, even as she sought to infuse him with hope.

He hugged her against his chest as if wanting to pull her inside him. When he eventually broke the kiss, he slid his mouth across her cheek and whispered into her hair, "You might not want to do that in a minute."

She couldn't imagine not wanting him. She needed his touch like she needed her heart to beat. "Then I'm glad I made the last time count."

He kissed her again, then lifted her back onto her stool and he rose. "You're making this personal when I was trying to be professional."

This was part of his military training—separate yourself from the messy job you had to do.

"But it *is* personal," she pointed out. "Why pretend?"

"You're right. It is." His gaze moved to hers and held. "The volleyball trophy that was stolen was kept in Susan Wells's house, the mother of the winning team's captain. Her son, Cal, has been living there since his divorce. Your brother delivered meals from the church to both her and Mrs. Jackson in the days before the thefts. He's the only common link I've found between the two cases. I have to question him."

Andrea blinked. It took a minute to absorb the onslaught of information.

Finn? He thought Finn was the thief?

She pressed her hand against her chest in an effort to soothe the ache in her heart. "You think Finn stole Mrs. Jackson's tea set?"

"I don't know. He's the only person who delivered meals to both women."

Rising, she turned away from him. Her thoughts were so scattered, so full of opposing emotions, she wasn't sure which one to grab on to. For the moment, anger worked. "So the ex in ex-con is irrelevant," she said when she calmed down enough to face him.

"He has a history. He's *linked.*"

"It's coincidence. Come on, Tyler, the beach volleyball trophy? How ridiculous."

"These thefts point to a young offender. Crimes of convenience, like the thief doesn't know what the items are worth, but they look shiny and expensive, so he takes them."

"Like a car?" She ground her teeth when he simply stared at her. "Maybe your thief is really clever. Maybe this guy took the trophy to confuse the efforts to find the tea set."

She could tell he hadn't thought of that possibility. She

wondered if he'd thought at all. Closing this case with Finn as the convenient, guilty party would wrap everything up nicely before the election.

"Finn is young, not stupid," she stated.

"I still have to talk to him."

"Officially?"

"Yes," he said miserably. "I'm sorry, but yes."

She glared at him, and he'd been exactly right—she had no desire to kiss him again. "He's my brother."

"I don't know him."

"You know me."

"You believe in him. You're his sister. You're supposed to. But I swore an oath to the people of Palmer's Island."

"Serve and protect?" she asked, her tone mocking. "And trust no one."

"Andrea, please." He held out his hands. "This is my job."

"Are you going to arrest him?"

He hesitated a second. "Not at this time."

"Should I call his lawyer?"

"That's up to you. I have to record his statement. We can do it here if you like."

She knew Finn had done nothing wrong, and no matter how betrayed she felt by Tyler, she was also sure he wasn't doing this simply to get elected. He wouldn't arrest her brother without hard evidence. Which he wouldn't find, since Finn was innocent.

But nobody could accuse her of stupidity. She wanted someone besides her on Finn's side. After calling her brother's cell phone and asking him to come to her house right away, she called Carr.

Though he reminded her he wasn't a criminal attorney, he agreed to come over. As she laid the phone in the cradle, she let herself mourn the opposing sides she and Tyler were now standing on.

"I thought Hamilton was a civil litigation attorney," Tyler said from behind her.

"He is." Turning, she crossed her arms over her chest and leaned back against the counter. "But how do you know that?"

"It's a small island."

A smooth answer. But Andrea knew it was an exaggeration. In her job, whenever a fake masqueraded as the real thing, she felt a prickling along her spine. She felt it now.

Tyler had asked somebody about Carr. After seeing him with her last night, he was either curious enough or jeal—

"You ran him."

His face was blank. "Excuse me?"

"Carr." She walked toward Tyler, watching his face closely. "You used the computers at the sheriff's office to click and point your way through his official records. You wanted to find out more about him." Somehow furious and flattered, she leaned against the bar. *"I'm not sharing."*

At least he didn't pretend not to remember his own words. His blue gaze burned into hers. "That's right."

"But you don't trust me, either."

"Of course I trust you."

"You think my brother's a thief."

He shook his head. "I don't think anything yet. I have evidence that suggests he might be involved."

"You have a coincidence."

"So far on this case that's *all* I have. I've got to start somewhere." He speared his hand through his hair in obvious frustration. "Would you rather I ignored the connection, or covered it up?"

The sister in her wanted him to do just that, but the practical woman, the professional who took pride in her own work, knew that wasn't possible. "I guess not."

She walked across the kitchen, looking out the windows along the back wall. Whenever she was feeling lousy, that sight could always make her smile. Today, she only felt an uneasy churning in her stomach like when the endless tide stirred the bottom of the sea.

Soon, Tyler joined her. "Why'd you call Hamilton?"

"He was the first person I thought of."

"I'd rather you think of me."

She turned her incredulous gaze on him. "You're the one standing here with the questions."

"Do you think I like this? Do you think I like upsetting you? Calling your brother in for questioning? I *have* to. This is my job."

"And it's important enough to cause this division between us?" she asked, even though she knew the accusation underlying it wasn't fair.

"My family expects the best," was his surprising answer.

"What—"

The doorbell interrupted any further questions, but she promised herself she'd get back to the topic of family and duty very soon.

Carr pulled her close for a hug the second she opened the door. "Are you sure you don't want to call Spencer?"

"I will if you think this is starting to go badly."

He laid his hands on her shoulders and studied her face. Apparently satisfied with what he saw, he nodded. "Deal."

Footsteps echoed in the hall behind her. "Who's Spencer?" Tyler asked.

Andrea turned to face her lover, knowing her friend had her back. "Finn's defense attorney."

Tyler shook hands with Carr, though the move was stiff and clearly forced.

There was some satisfaction in knowing Tyler liked Carr being in her house even less than she liked her brother being questioned by the police.

The men sat at the kitchen table, and Andrea poured out glasses of iced tea simply to have something to do with her hands. She and Finn had built an unshakable bond of trust. With Spencer and Sister Mary Katherine's help, they'd surrounded him with a new kind of family, replacing the brutal codependency of the gang.

He wouldn't risk all that.

And if he had, she'd kick his ass all the way back to jail personally.

"Is Finn under arrest?" Carr asked, his dark gaze focused on Tyler's.

"Not at this time," Tyler returned.

"And the only evidence you have is the fact that he was in both homes prior to the thefts."

"Yes."

"No fingerprints near where the items were taken?"

"I still need Dwayne's report from Cal's place, but no."

"No witnesses to the break-ins?"

"No."

Carr's teeth flashed in a hard smile. "You don't have much, do you?"

"Not really, no," Tyler said casually, though nobody in the room took his tone as anything less than serious. And the authority behind his words, as well as the resentment in his eyes, clearly communicated his resolve.

"Andy!" a familiar voice called from the foyer. "What's so—"

Her brother stopped as he rounded the corner to the kitchen and noticed the gathering around the table.

Wearing baggy jeans and a white T-shirt, his short, spiky blond hair kissed by the sun, he looked even younger than his twenty years. Only as she watched his hazel eyes narrow, responding to Tyler's uniform and slow rise to his feet, did she remember he'd spent his high school years swallowed by violence and nearly two years in prison.

She walked toward him, wrapping her arms around his lean waist. Her head fit neatly under his chin. "Deputy Landry needs to ask you a few questions," she said calmly as she tried to bely the anxiety she felt.

"About?"

He was vibrating with uncertainty, and after everything he'd been through, she feared subjecting him to the humiliation of this more than anything. "Can I have a few minutes alone with him?" she asked, turning toward Tyler.

Tyler indicated the chair across from him. "I really—"

"Yes, you can," Carr said, sending Tyler a glare as he stood. "Why don't the three of us go out to the deck?"

Finn's gaze shifted from Carr, to Tyler, then to Andrea. "Whatever."

Without looking at Tyler, Andrea took her brother's hand and led him and Carr outside.

"I didn't take Mrs. Jackson's tea set," Finn said the moment they stepped into the breezy sunshine.

Andrea whirled on him. "How did you know why Tyler was here?"

"Something's missing." His shoulders jerked in a shrug. "Ex-con right around the corner."

Andrea cast a glance at Carr. "We don't think you took anything."

Hunching his shoulders, Finn shoved his hands in the front pockets of his jeans. "But the cops do?"

Just the introduction her only family needed to the man she'd been sleeping with. "Not necessarily. Tyler is a... friend. We went to high school together."

"You're not under arrest," Carr added. "You simply need to answer the deputy's questions." Carr laid his hand on Finn's shoulder. "Be honest, but don't offer any information he doesn't ask for."

"Like?" Andrea asked, not sure what Carr meant herself.

"Did you go out last night after work?" Carr asked Finn.

"Sure. Some buddies and I went to Mabel's for burgers, then we—"

Carr held up his hand to stop him. "The answer to the question I asked you is *yes.* That's it. Don't elaborate unless there's a follow-up question. Now, did you go out last night?"

Looking wary, Finn nodded. "Yes."

"Excellent. Where did you go?"

"Mabel's."

Carr ran him through a few more questions, asking him about the nights before both the tea set and trophy went missing. He asked him if he'd done anything to violate his parole in the last month.

Thankfully, the clear answer to that was no. Unfortunately, Finn's alibis—and, dear heaven, Andrea couldn't believe that word was even in question—weren't great. The night before the tea set had been found missing, he'd been in his apartment on the church grounds, reading and watching TV. He hadn't talked to or been visited by anyone. He swore he hadn't broken his curfew, though.

Last night, though he'd helped Sister Mary Katherine with the youth sleepover, he'd actually slept in his apartment, not in the gym with the kids. The sister hadn't felt it appropriate to have a young, single male as an overnight chaperone for teenage girls.

Andrea felt much calmer after Carr's coaching even though she had no idea where any of them would stand after the questioning. She tried to stifle the selfish thoughts that flooded her brain.

Why did this have to happen between her and Tyler at such a delicate place in the relationship they'd started to build? Last night he'd known she was the high school math nerd, and he'd wanted her anyway. She'd felt treasured, sexy and powerful in his arms. How would they now breach the chasm between them? Would they even want to?

"Is this guy more than a friend, Andy?" her brother asked suddenly.

"What guy?" she asked, pretending ignorance while hiding a wince.

Finn stabbed his finger toward the French doors, through which they could clearly see Tyler pacing by the kitchen table. "That guy."

"We'll talk about it later. You really weren't out past midnight this week, were you?"

"No, Mom," Finn answered on a sigh.

Andrea wrapped her arm around his waist as they headed inside. "Hey, pal, it isn't me you have to answer to on that point. It's Sister Mary Katherine."

Finn scowled. "Yeah. Like I'm dumb enough to disobey her."

"HAVE A SEAT, Mr. Hastings," Tyler said firmly, but gently, to his suspect.

His girlfriend's brother.

Hell, could he even call her his girlfriend? They had a tenuous bond—in bed. Outside their cocoon of closeness, however, they seemed to rarely agree, and right then, they stood on opposite sides of a deep ravine of suspicion and disappointment.

To think he'd made fun of crime on his sleepy hometown island. Rose and palmetto bush vandals would be welcomed with open arms at the moment. Anything that didn't involve the woman he…

Well, the woman he had the hots for and wanted to be with, glaring at him as if he was a particularly pesky bug she needed to squash.

He ran through the pertinent questions about both thefts with Finn, easily noticing a lawyer's touch in the coaching. It was his right, so Tyler had no issue with the consultation. Still, he couldn't help wondering if this could be cleared up much quicker without the protective hovering of Carr Hamilton.

But maybe that was simply a personal bias.

"Did you take Mrs. Jackson's silver tea set?" he asked, forcing himself not to glance at Andrea.

"No, sir."

"Did you ever touch it?"

"No, sir. She kept it—" He stopped after a quick glance at Hamilton. "I didn't touch it."

"But you know where she kept the set," Tyler pressed.

After a short hesitation, Finn nodded. "Yes, sir."

"Where did she keep it?"

"In a glass cabinet in the den."

"How did you notice it was there? Did you admire it?"

Finn let out a barking laugh. "No."

Tyler braced his hand on the kitchen table and leaned toward Finn. "How, Mr. Hastings?"

His gaze, which had just enough green to mark him as related to Andrea, met Tyler's and held. "She bragged about it. She was mostly background noise, you know? But she loved that stupid tea set, 'cause she went on and on about it until some of the stuff sunk in."

"And what sunk in?"

"It belonged to Andrew Jackson. The president," he clarified with an uncertain look around. "He took it with him to the White House."

When he stopped, Tyler prompted, "Anything else?"

After a long pause, Finn stared at the floor. "It was priceless."

Hamilton rose. "That's enough. If you have follow-up questions, Deputy, you can arrange them at another time. Mr. Hastings has been more than cooperative with this abrupt request for an interview."

"So have I, Counselor," Tyler returned, putting some heat in his tone. "Two thefts inside a week is practically a crime spree for Palmer's Island. I could have insisted on calling him to the station. I didn't, out of respect for Andrea."

Hamilton nodded, then not-so-subtly nudged him toward the front door. "We have full confidence that you'll bring this…*spree*—" he seemed to be amused by the word "—to a satisfactory end."

"And I will." Before Hamilton could open the door and shove Tyler outside, he planted his feet, crossing his arms over his chest. "I'd like to talk to Andrea."

"I suggest you call—"

"Thanks, Carr," Andrea said as she appeared at the end of the hall. "I have a few things to say to Deputy Landry."

"Of course." Hamilton nodded in that calm, elegant way of his that set Tyler's teeth on edge. "Finn and I will go out on the back deck and give you some privacy."

After a quick murmuring, Tyler heard the back door open, then close. Andrea said nothing during that time. She leaned against the foyer wall, her gaze fixed on his face.

"That was lousy," she said.

He was pretty sure she wasn't talking about her friend Carr Hamilton's hand brushing down her arm before he'd turned away. For Tyler, however, that image was burned into his memory like a brand. "I'm sorry," he said, fighting to focus on his job.

"Did you have to be so cold?"

"I had to be professional. I have a duty to honor—much as that sounds goofy and old-fashioned."

"It doesn't. This is just…" She trailed off, lifting her hands, then letting them drop, obviously not knowing what *this* was.

Unfortunately, Tyler didn't, either. He wanted to touch her, but she seemed much farther away than the physical distance where she stood. He'd fought battles, flew through hostile skies, parachuted onto beaches in the blackened night, knowing daylight might bring his death.

But he didn't know how to fight this.

How did he honor his commitments and not ruin everything he wanted to have with Andrea?

"I don't want my brother part of this investigation," she said finally.

"I'm sorry. He is."

"Do you believe he answered your questions truthfully?"

"Yes."

"Because he's my brother, and I believe him, or because you think he's innocent?"

He hesitated a second, uncertain whether the truth would help or hurt. "I'm not sure."

She dropped her gaze and turned away. "Let me know when you decide."

He grabbed her arm. "I'm sorry. The last thing I want to do is upset you."

"And I'm sorry, but I'll do whatever I have to in order to protect my brother. He's paid for his mistakes, and I won't have him doubted by anybody." Her eyes darkened with regret. "Even you."

8

CARRYING A SCREAMING HEADACHE direct from Andrea's into the police station, Tyler caught sight of two people who made him want to turn around and go right back out again.

Lester Cradock, his opponent in the election for sheriff, paced beside Aqua's glassed-in office. His trademark bullwhip—he was a staunch gun-control advocate—was hooked to his belt loop and snapped against his skinny leg with each step.

The other occupant of the room was his mother. She was sitting in a chair, campaign posters and a book in her lap. Probably the latest volume of crossword puzzles. Solving every last one was part of her grand plan for avoiding Alzheimer's.

He loved her, of course, and he wanted to be sheriff, but he needed to concentrate on his cases. He had to prove Finn Hastings guilty—and destroy his closeness with Andrea—or he had to dismiss him and find the real thief. Maybe saving his career *and* his love life.

When he felt so close to failing, he didn't need the reminder that he was expected to live up to his family's sterling reputation.

"*There* you are, honey," his mother said, rising and scooting toward him.

"Hi, Mama." He kissed her cheek and tried to look pleased to see her. "You look pretty today."

Her face flushed. "You always know just the right—"

"Deputy!" Lester called, marching over. "I have some important town matters to discuss with you. Can't the personal business wait?"

"Lester," Tyler began in a smooth tone, belying his annoyance at the other man's rude interruption, "do you know my mother, Sophia Landry?"

"Yes, ma'am," he said with forced politeness. "But since I don't suppose I can count on your vote in two weeks, I won't give you one of my manifestos on the changes that need to be immediately instated to our island's archaic justice system."

Tyler's mother smiled, sweet as the seven generations of Southern belle that flowed through her veins. "And I am most thankful for that gracious reality."

Lester frowned, apparently uncertain whether or not he'd been insulted.

Cheered, Tyler took his mother's arm and led her away. "This won't take long, Lester. Why don't you have a seat in the meantime?"

Back in the sheriff's office, he offered his mom coffee and the seat in front of the desk. "Mama, as much as I appreciate you handling Lester, I need to talk to him to get rid of him, so I can get back to work. Maybe I could come by the house later on?"

"That's fine, dear." She smoothed her hands down her flowered skirt. "I only wanted to bring you some more campaign posters." She laid the stack on his desk, then leaned back, undoubtedly about to launch into the real reason she'd come. There were posters on every pole, window and bulletin board on the island. "You might be interested to know that a reporter at the newspaper has already called both your father and I, *and* your grandfather, wanting to know if we think you can handle the responsibilities of sheriff."

Tyler barely resisted the urge to drop his head into his hands. "The island newspaper?" he asked, wondering how far the humiliation planned to spread.

"Yes. This reporter went on a rant about some missing silver. He'd apparently talked to Cal Wells this morning, who's upset about his volleyball trophy."

Tyler held up his hand to forestall the rest of the explanation. "I know, Mama. I'm on it."

"Of course I told this idiotic busybody reporter that you could handle the responsibilities of being sheriff just fine. Honestly." She let out a huff of disgust. "You're a lieutenant in the United States Navy. A decorated officer, first-rate pilot and hero to your unit."

"I appreciate your confidence, but I doubt Cal or Mrs. Jackson care about my military record. They just want their stuff back."

"You'll be a wonderful sheriff." She reached across the desk and patted his hand. "Just like your grandfather."

He hadn't shared any of the trauma of leaving the Navy with his mother. He hadn't told her he doubted his ability to lead and serve his community, and he couldn't bring himself to share his uncertainties now. Greatness had followed every step of his life. She didn't have to know about his single misstep. "I'll do my best, Mama."

Rising, she walked around the desk and kissed his cheek. "Make sure you get your hair cut before the swearing-in ceremony. I want some nice pictures of you and your grandfather in your uniforms."

Victory was a foregone conclusion.

Wasn't it?

After escorting his mother outside, he reluctantly called Lester back to the office. He poured himself a fresh cup of coffee and took two aspirin as he listened to the other man ramble on about campaign reform—he was in favor. Dolphin poaching—he was against.

The guy had passion, Tyler would give him that. Unfortunately, the fact that campaigns on the island consisted of a debate at the rotary club and a few hundred posters stapled to telephone poles and bulletin boards was lost on Lester. The reality of legal jurisdictions had also escaped his notice. The Coast Guard pretty much had a lock on the safeguarding of marine life.

He was considering personally financing Lester's bid for Congress—then Washington could deal with him rather than his fellow islanders—when he barked out, "Did you look at my proposal on banning guns? Despite the fact that we're opponents, I think if we both came out strongly in favor of the policy, the citizens would respond."

Tyler sighed. "Lester, while I agree guns have no business in the hands of kids or inexperienced users, they're a pretty crucial piece of equipment for a cop."

"But they *shouldn't* be," Lester asserted, his beady eyes narrowed.

"And maybe someday somebody will invent something better. Till then we use what we've got."

Smirking, Lester held up his whip. "I've got this."

"Can you flick that thing faster than a bullet shot out of a nine millimeter pistol?"

"Hmm..."

"When you can, we'll talk."

After that serious blow of physics, Tyler managed to get Lester out of the office. Alone and leaning back in his chair, he ran through the theft cases one by one. Eyes closed, he pictured the actual crimes, trying to line up the facts with his thoughts and instincts.

And something was plain down screwy.

Especially when he tried to cast Finn Hastings as the culprit.

If he knew Mrs. Jackson's silver was priceless—and he'd admitted he did—he also had to know fencing such a piece wouldn't be easy. And no way would he consider using his sister to help him. He had to know she'd never do so.

Neither could Tyler picture Finn helping himself to the volleyball trophy. If he was tempted to take anything, there was probably plenty of easily sold jewelry around. He'd confirm that when Dwayne returned, but the Wells house was easily worth two million dollars. It followed that they'd filled it with valuable things. Things that could be shoved in a pocket without detection.

Instead, the thief had broken in the house in the middle of the night and taken a worthless, three-foot-tall trophy?

He couldn't make the scene play in his head.

What had happened, however, he couldn't say. He only knew one thing at this point. His life would never be back on track until he'd closed these cases.

He'd wanted—needed, really—a break from balls-to-the-wall military action. He'd come home to find the reasons he'd gone off to fight in the first place. His feelings for Andrea were a living, breathing reminder of beauty and purity, the core of defending God and country.

Semper Fidelis. Always faithful.

She embodied the phrase that wasn't just a slogan, but a way of life. Her defense of her brother demonstrated her strength, character and loyalty.

He was so damn crazy about her.

"Sir, I've got the evidence from the Wells house," Dwayne said as he walked into the office.

Determined to get answers for his fellow islanders, as well as—hopefully—repair his relationship with Andrea, Tyler rose. "Let's get to it."

BY SUNSET, TYLER HAD parked his SUV in the church parking lot near the side of the old orphanage.

He was doing his duty and possibly betraying his lover, but he didn't see how they could move forward, or how he'd get elected, if he didn't find out who was responsible for the thefts.

Even if the guilty party was her brother.

Finn walked down the sidewalk a few minutes later and got into one of the church vans. Tyler followed him at a discrete distance as he headed toward town.

Surely, if he was set on nefarious business, he wouldn't do so in a church van? But then the whole reason suspicion had fallen on Finn in the first place was because he'd delivered meals to the elderly for a church-sponsored program.

The younger man drove smoothly, without speeding, to the ice cream shop just around the corner from the historic buildings of city hall.

While Tyler parked in front of the souvenir shop nearby, he watched Finn order a giant sundae, talk with some of the teens who were hanging out and have a brief conversation in the shadows of a palm with a pretty brunette.

Finn left after talking to the girl, presumably, by the route he took, heading back to the church. Andrea had mentioned a curfew, and it appeared her brother adhered to it.

Since tourist season had waned, it was hard for Tyler to put cars between him and Finn or to keep a discrete distance without calling attention to himself, and he couldn't help but think that if Finn was the thief he was pretty damn calm about it.

Moments later, Finn made an abrupt move and pulled off the side of the road.

Even as he wondered if the guy had car trouble, Tyler had no choice but to roll past him. Had Finn spotted the tail? Had he gotten a call from the cute brunette?

While Tyler considered the ideas and looked for a place to turn around and double-back, lights suddenly flashed in his rearview mirror.

Finn.

When Tyler glanced back, the young man waved.

Shaking his head at his gullibility, Tyler pulled over in the post office parking lot. Finn had spent time in prison. He was in a gang before that. Despite getting caught, he certainly had plenty of street smarts.

As Tyler exited his vehicle, he saw Finn do the same.

The other man raised his hands, then crossed them over his narrow chest and leaned back onto the front grill of the van. "Did you need to talk to me, Deputy?"

"I already did."

"And I guess I didn't convince you with my answers."

"I have to be sure."

"You like my sister."

Tyler didn't flinch at the abrupt question and also didn't

bother to ask how Finn knew of his feelings. He imagined they were pretty obvious to everybody. "Very much," he said simply.

"Does that mean you're going to let me off?"

Tyler looked into eyes that weren't the same vibrant color as Andrea's but had the same steely determination, and realized he wanted to make her happy more than he wanted to solve this case. "Have you done anything you'd like to confess?"

"Father Dominick handles confessions."

The kid was smart like his sister, too. Tyler just hoped he was innocent. "Have you done anything that would require me to arrest you?"

"No, sir, but sometimes that doesn't matter when you're one of the only ex-felons on an island this small."

"It does to me."

Tyler let Finn go and drove home, brooding about the case and certainly about being caught tailing a suspect.

Trudging inside his rented house a mere block from the beach, he glanced around at the leased furniture and wondered if he belonged here. The island was his home, always would be in his heart, but he'd spent so much of his time on the road, he wondered if he had the commitment to settle down.

He tossed his keys on the kitchen table and headed for his bedroom, though he doubted he'd sleep. If Finn was the thief, he wasn't sure he could arrest him. Another conviction would send the kid back to prison for a long, long time. Could he have that on his conscience? Then again, how could he not solve the crime? What kind of would-be sheriff did that make him?

Sheriff Caldwell would be back in ten days; the election would be held in two weeks. So, he certainly didn't have long to decide where his loyalties lied.

THE NEXT MORNING, AFTER little sleep, Tyler walked into the station with his sunglasses on and his third cup of coffee in his hand.

And he was no closer to solving the thefts.

His tailing of Finn Hastings had been a disaster, so he was no closer to learning whether the kid had gone back to his old ways or not.

The results from the fingerprint evidence on the Wells house that he and Dwayne had processed the afternoon before basically matched those from the Jackson scene. Prints everywhere. The victims dominated. The others from the Jackson home had been eliminated as the cleaning service, and since the Wellses didn't use the same service, they still had to process those prints before determining who they belonged to.

None of the prints, so far, belonged to anybody who had a criminal record. Unless Tyler counted Cal's misdemeanor conviction for streaking when he attended the College of Charleston over twenty years before.

And not only did Tyler not count Cal's past as a trend toward breaking the law, he'd been forced to put it out of his mind in favor of two other, more immediate problems.

One, the extremely short, emotionless quote he'd given to a newspaper reporter who'd wanted a comment about the case. He didn't see how he could change what he'd said, but would his constituents wonder if he cared at all? Maybe he'd been professional, but also distant. Did he even deserve the job?

Especially given problem number two: how long would it be before Finn told his sister about last night's surveillance? And how long after that before she threw him out of her life?

At least the paper only came out once every two weeks.

Wincing as the station house door banged shut behind him, he crossed the blessedly empty lobby and saw Aqua already sitting at her desk, flipping through the ever-present fashion magazine. "Mornin'," he said briefly as he passed her.

"Glad you didn't put a *good* in front of that greeting, boss."

He paused. "How is today already bad? It just started."

She tossed aside her magazine and held up a newspaper. "And it's all downhill from here."

Squinting, he leaned toward her. The headline Serial Silver Stealer On The Loose blared from the front page. His stomach churned as he took the paper from her hand.

"Say that three times fast," she commented, obviously amused and annoyed at the same time.

"What happened to the biweekly schedule?" he asked incredulously as he scanned down to his picture in his Navy dress whites.

"They printed a special edition."

"How proactive."

His single quote—*We're using the full resources of the sheriff's department in order to bring the perpetrators of these crimes to justice*—was highlighted in a bold box of text. But the rest of the article was riddled with innuendos about his ability to replace the island's beloved Sheriff Caldwell. The reporter even speculated that Tyler thought the job of sheriff was beneath him after all his glories and triumphs in the Marines.

A moment of guilt moved within him as he read that. Maybe he did consider coming home a demotion, or at least a setback. Maybe he considered the case a distraction from his pursuit of Andrea.

But that didn't mean he wasn't doing his best. It didn't mean he wouldn't solve the case or get the stolen items back or arrest the guilty party.

He just might not do it with his whole heart.

Tossing the paper back to Aqua, he turned toward the door. "I'll be in the sheriff's office."

"It'll be yours soon," she said casually, her attention already back on her magazine.

"That's looking less and less likely, but thanks for the support."

"I'm only supporting you 'cause you're cuter than Lester, you know."

He was sure she was kidding. Well, pretty sure. "Gee, there's something every town needs—a cute sheriff."

"Doesn't hurt." With a red marker, she circled something on her magazine. "Oh, and you have a visitor in your office."

Picturing reporters, Sister Mary Katherine and the stern leader of an island protest group all in one blink, Tyler ground to a halt. "Who?"

"Telling would be ruining the surprise." She glanced over her shoulder. "Go on. Don't be a chicken."

"I'm not—" Setting his jaw, he shoved open the door to the hall. "If I don't like this surprise, I'm kicking you and your magazines out on your asses."

She snorted. "Sure you will."

Determined not to delay the inevitable confrontation with his mystery guest, Tyler gulped coffee as he walked down the hall. As he rounded the doorway, he pulled off his sunglasses. "Look, I don't know—"

Certain he was hallucinating, he squeezed his eyes shut. Could sleep deprivation and a caffeine overdose cause delusions? He was sure there'd been some important information about those possibilities in his military training.

"Hey there, Deputy."

He opened his eyes.

Andrea Hastings was still there, sitting on the sheriff's battered desk, her long, slender legs bare and perfect as they dangled over the edge. Wearing a white sundress and tiny pink sweater, he completely lost the power of speech as he entertained the fantasy of ripping that dress from her body and burying all his worries, confusion and uncertainty in her soft, welcoming body.

Smiling, she held up the newspaper. "Thought you could use some help on this silver theft thing."

Sure he could. But the only nonsensual thought pounding through his brain was short and simple.

Aqua was getting a raise.

HE LOOKED TIRED.

Some small part of Andrea wanted to be glad he was suffering, since she was, too. Not to mention Finn's state of mind at the moment.

But she couldn't hold that petty thought for long. Someone with a thing for silver, or just things in general, was putting them through this mess. So she was firmly on the side of justice—and making sure her brother's name was cleared in the process.

"You're here," Tyler said, looking both pleased and shocked.

"I'm a little surprised myself. I was going to e-mail the information I found out about Mrs. Jackson's tea set." She tossed the newspaper on the desk behind her. "Then I read that bunch of garbage by Jerry Mescle and decided to come right over."

"Oh."

The expression of longing on his face made her shift nervously. "He—Jerry Mescle, that is—went off to Hollywood to make documentaries, if you remember, but he came back almost immediately to write for the *Herald*. He thought everybody in California was fake. Can you imagine?"

Tyler set his travel coffee mug on the filing cabinet by the door, then took a step toward her. "He never did like me."

"Jerry Mescle never liked anybody. And nobody liked him right back. Even geeks like me avoided him."

Tyler closed the distance between them, stopping so close she had to drop her head back to meet his gaze. "You weren't a geek," he told her.

"Sure I was." Trying to ignore the flutter of nerves, she smiled. "And damn proud of it. We rule the world, you know."

"I know. Us jocks just defend it."

"And look really good doing it."

He inched even closer, and her heartbeat sped up. "It's the uniform."

She swallowed. "No, I really don't think it is."

Reaching out, he cupped her jaw in his palm. "I'm really glad you're here."

As he leaned down, clearly intent on kissing her, she leaped off the desk and darted away from him. "I think maybe we should keep things, you know, professional between us."

"You think maybe you know?" His lips turned up, he raised his eyebrows. "Since you're so decisive, you mind telling me why?"

Because I like you too much.

Since there was no way she was admitting that, she cleared her throat. "We're standing on opposites sides of this issue. You want to arrest my brother and I—"

"Okay, I followed him last night because that's my job, and if you have to know, I hated doing it, because I knew it would hurt you, but I'm..." He paused. Obviously he'd noted the shocked expression on her face. "You don't know anything about last night."

She glared at him. "Well, goodness, no, Lieutenant," she said in a deliberately sweet tone that contradicted her disappointment. "I'd love to hear all about it, though."

So he told her. The description of Finn recognizing the tail and coming up behind Tyler drained her anger. This case was testing everybody's patience and sense of duty. She wasn't sure how much she could trust Tyler with her heart, but she had confidence he'd do what was right otherwise.

"I think we can both agree that I don't *want* to arrest your brother," he included. "I'll arrest him only if the evidence warrants me doing so."

"You won't find the evidence."

"Then you have nothing to worry about."

She shook her head. "It's more than that. You suspect him. I don't want him to be suspected. We both need to be objective and fair while we find the truth."

"I agree."

You do? Just like that he was fine with keeping his distance? Was she so easily dismissed? Didn't he think the heat between them was, well…hot? Then again, wasn't that what she wanted? Didn't they need to slow down? Didn't they need to reevaluate just how—

He startled her from her internal argument by wrapping his arms around her waist. "I can be objective and fair on the case and still touch you as often and as thoroughly as possible every single second I'm not working on the objective and fair resolution of our mutual problem."

That was some reevaluation.

"Okay," she said, off balance both mentally and physically.

He kissed her cheek, nuzzled down her neck. "Okay, you agree I can be objective, or okay you're going to help me solve this case?"

"Ah, well…" Dear heaven, he had amazing lips. Ripples of sensual awareness flowed down her spine, pooling between her legs. "Both, I guess."

She could feel his smile against her skin. "Remind me to have every serious discussion with you just like this."

"Mmm…okay."

His lips found his way to hers. He nibbled, then ran his tongue slowly, inch by inch, along her lower lip. His scent was all spicy male, and he tasted even better.

Hold on. Serious discussion?

"Back up, buster." She waggled her finger. "This is exactly what I'm talking about. We do need to have a serious discussion about this case—mainly how to keep my brother out of jail."

All innocence, he extended his arms. "I'm ready when you are."

"Then sit there." She pointed behind the sheriff's desk.

When he'd safely moved behind that solid piece of oak, she slid into the visitor's chair on the opposite side. "So, about the Jackson tea set. My contacts haven't seen or heard anything about the tea set so far. They promised to discreetly ask around."

He frowned. "These are your *criminal* contacts?"

"They prefer the term alternative-income architects."

"I bet they do. Discreet, huh? I don't want the thief scared off."

"Did I mention these guys are never caught?"

"I think you did."

"Don't you think it's significant that the tea set hasn't shown up anywhere? Why steal something valuable, then not attempt to make a profit?"

"Maybe the thief is laying low, waiting for time to pass."

"If he wanted to pull off a low-key crime, he picked a lousy victim and item to steal."

"Exactly. This goes back to my theory about an unsophisticated thief, one unfamiliar with the value of the items he's taken."

Unsophisticated like a kid. Like Finn, she thought, but didn't say. Even if Finn was considered young in years, his time in prison had aged him, hardened him and certainly made him smarter than this silver-stealing fool. "Or one whose motive isn't the theft at all."

He looked justifiably confused. "A thief's motive is usually to steal something."

Glad she could finally lead him to her theory, she leaned forward. "How badly does Lester Cradock want to win this election?"

"Lester?" Tyler's eyes narrowed. "Nobody takes him seriously. He takes himself *very* seriously. What does he have to do with—" He stopped, then shook his head as her implication apparently occurred to him. "Lester didn't steal anything. He's an activist, not a thief."

"Never seen an activist arrested, have you?"

"Sure. For their cause. Trophies and tea sets aren't his cause."

"But winning this election is. These thefts are casting you in a bad light. Are you trying to tell me you aren't worried? If you don't solve these crimes by election day, which is less than two weeks from today, you think you'll still be sheriff? Don't you think the timing is significant?"

"Of course I'm concerned," he said, his tone casual, even though his eyes were dark with focused intensity. "I want people to have confidence in me and believe I can assume Sheriff Caldwell's place. But I'm definitely not worried about Lester."

"Why not?"

"He doesn't really want to get elected. He just wants his ideas to be heard. Kind of like the third- or fourth-party candidate in a presidential election."

"Are you willing to stake the outcome of this case on that assumption?"

"Are you reaching for any suspect to move suspicion off your brother?"

"No." But that was a pretty good strategy, come to think of it. "I want this over."

"I do, too. But I have to investigate with an even hand. I have to explore every possibility."

"This is a possibility."

"Technically, so is your brother."

"So we're still standing on opposite sides."

"We don't have to."

She looked away. "It sure feels like it."

And this, this right here, was the problem with one-night stands, getting close too early, having sex and not a relationship. They had heat and chemistry and fun, but no true trust. He was her fantasy; she was his fascination. Beyond that, they had no history to build on.

Did she even want to build?

He meant too much—to her past and present. But the future was murky.

She knew Sloan would tell her to just go for it, to enjoy and not worry about tomorrow. Andrea, though, had spent most of her life involved in insurance. Worrying about tomorrow was her business.

And yet her passion and emotions were mired in the past.

If there was any hope of holding on to the wonder and thrill she felt only when she and Tyler were together, they had to find a way to breach their trust issues outside the case.

"We'll figure it out together," Tyler said quietly. "Your brains and my badge?"

Hope punched through her spirits. "I can't think of a better combination."

9

"SO WHAT DID YOU think of the speech?"

Sitting by the fire in the Dolphin Club's den, Andrea glanced over at the familiar voice, the words delivered in a husky tone as warm as the flames beside her.

Tyler walked toward her. He was wearing his khaki sheriff's department uniform, a sight she'd never failed to appreciate.

She rose, a bit unsteady, still holding a glass of deep red wine somebody had handed her during the after-dinner speech. The blaze in the stone-covered hearth fought off the unexpected late-October chill that had been in the air all afternoon.

A chill that fled the closer he came—and had nothing to do with the fire.

She was at full-fledged war with herself about him. She wanted him, yet she feared the feelings he inspired. "You want some wine?" she asked, extending her glass.

"I bet the Dolphins have some whiskey stocked around here."

He strode toward the far side of the room, which was filled with old books, dark woods and antique bowls and vases. They were surprisingly alone in the cozy room, though she could hear voices from the party in the grand hall next door.

The Dolphins had class and style, like an old English gentleman's club. They also, apparently, had whiskey, since Tyler came back with a heavy crystal tumbler containing a small measure of amber liquid.

"Your speech was wonderful," she said, raising her own glass in a toast.

He tapped his glass against hers, and the crystal sang. "You were the inspiration."

He'd talked about second chances and second glances. And while at first she'd thought he was talking about people like Finn, she realized quickly his heart had been talking to her.

His bright, blue gaze fixed on her face, he glided his hand down her arm and grasped her hand. "You want to sit?"

Resting beside him on the sofa, she sipped her wine and watched the fire. After all the turmoil over the last couple of days, it was nice to simply sit with him and know they had a common goal. To know that he respected, admired and desired her. There was a time in her life when she wouldn't have dreamed for more.

Still, there was so much unsettled between them—her London trip, his election, the past and her insecurities.

A wily silver thief.

Staring into his glass, he slid his thumb along the back of her hand. "I'm not big on commitment."

"That's not true. You served your country. You've come home to serve your community. That sounds like commitment to me."

He sipped his drink. "I've made mistakes, and my track record with relationships isn't very good."

"Mine, either." Deep down she knew she didn't want to gamble her heart. Opening her feelings the way she had to

Tyler when she was so young and having nothing—not even a decent kiss—to show for it had hardened her. She tried to pass off her own history with a shrug. "I get bored with relationships, or I don't even start them. My work was my life until I came home to watch over Finn."

"And why'd you do that?"

"Come home? He needed me. Why did you come back?"

"I needed it."

Not for the first time, Andrea sensed there was a great deal more to Tyler's early retirement than he'd said. *Family and duty.* "Did something happen?"

"I made a mistake. A job-related one," he clarified.

"That can be pretty serious if you're a Marine."

"Yes, it can." Regret filled his eyes when he turned toward her. "I thought we were talking about us."

"We will. This is more important right now."

He said nothing for a long moment. "I'm not what I seem."

"How's that?"

"I've killed."

"You were in the military for—"

He shook his head, stopping her. "That's not what I mean. My mistakes killed people."

He was serious—deadly serious to make a bad pun. Still, imagining Tyler doing something wrong didn't compute in her world. "How?"

"I—" He set down his whiskey glass on the mahogany table in front of them and rose, then walked toward the fire. "It's over. It doesn't have anything to do with you."

Heart pounding, she followed him. "You can still tell me."

"I can't. You expect the best, just like my family."

"I expect you to be you, and you are the best." When

he started to interrupt, she laid her hand on his arm and added, "No matter what mistakes you've made."

He remained rigid beside her. "I don't want to talk about it."

Andrea wanted to push. She wanted to know what had turned this fun-loving, charming guy dark and agonized. Yet she sensed she'd hit a wall. Finding a door—or at least a window—would require her to share part of herself. How could she expect him to divulge intimate details of his life when they shared nothing but their bodies? To reach him, she had to risk the heart she was so determined to protect.

The charismatic lover snapped back as quickly as he'd gone. He linked their hands. "We agree on the thefts—we want them solved. We agree we're crazy about each other."

She slipped her arms around his waist. "So I guess you're stuck with me."

He gathered her close against his chest. "Fine by me."

"At least until the election."

Leaning back, he studied her. "I barely get two weeks?"

"I start a special assignment in London the day after the election."

Shadows of regret moved across his face. "For how long?"

"Several weeks. Maybe longer. It depends on Finn."

"And the outcome of the case?"

Finn was innocent, and she could trust Tyler to uncover the truth of the theft. "I'm hoping that won't be a factor."

"Weeks, huh? That's a long time," he said. "I can't count on your brilliance to speed up the process?"

"Unfortunately not. I'm categorizing and certifying seventeenth-century paintings for a revision of an insurance policy for the National Portrait Gallery. Trust me, there wasn't much to do but paint back then."

"Sounds…"

She was used to the lack of enthusiasm for her historical projects. "Boring? Tedious?"

"Like it'll take a long time." He smiled and tugged her toward the back door. "We'd better get started."

On the deck, he pressed her against the building's exterior wall and kissed her as if his life depended on it.

Her heart leaped; her blood thickened with desire.

The sensations were instant and already familiar. She craved the feel of his skin heating hers, and she was completely kidding herself if she thought she could dabble in this bond between them.

She wouldn't get caught up in work and forget to call him. She wouldn't be able to leave for months, then come back and casually have dinner and catch up on his life. This was nothing like the relationships she'd had in the past. This meant much, much more.

Even though part of her wished it didn't.

Cupping her head and never breaking the kiss, he moved her to the corner of the deck, where he lifted her onto the wooden railing and moved between her legs. She wrapped her legs around his waist, and the delicious friction between his erection and the heat at the juncture of her thighs sent flames of need coursing through her body.

"Somebody might see us," she said in a token attempt to be sensible.

"It's dark," he mumbled against her cheek as he began unbuttoning the top of her sundress.

Earlier, she thought it was cold outside, but as his fingers slid into her bra and glided over her nipple, she felt a blast of heat.

She reached between them and released the button on his uniform pants, her thoughts completely focused on satisfying the ache as soon as possible, regardless of where they were.

Wrapping her hand around the hard length of his erection, she stroked him as he moved his hand underneath her dress. He teased her with his touch, only the tips of his fingers brushing her heat.

She went damp, and her belly contracted. "Tyler, please."

Thankfully, he obliged her by moving his fingers under the elastic edge of her panties, and with the unerring accuracy of a pilot found exactly the right button to press.

She groaned, stroking him as he did her. Their breathing became choppy.

Which was probably why it took a while for the ringing to register.

"You've *got* to be kidding," Tyler muttered as he pulled back and leaned his forehead against hers.

"What's going on?"

"It can't possibly be anything good." He fumbled for the phone in his pocket. After a quick glance at the screen, he pressed a kiss against her cheek. "It's the station. I have to answer."

"Sure." She grasped the railing and tried to balance herself and her thoughts. "I'll—"

"Don't move," he said, holding her in place. He pressed a button on the phone and the next voice she heard was Aqua Joliet's.

"We got a situation, boss."

"Don't we always?" Tyler answered, his tone lamenting.

"These days? Yeah."

"Aqua, is this going to be a regular thing with us?"

"Only for the next fifty years or so."

The matter-of-fact tone in the dispatcher's voice made Andrea smile, despite the lousy timing of the island's criminal element. And since when had that been a problem? Again, she wondered about the timing of all this trouble, the proximity to the election and the fact that the sheriff was on vacation.

"How fun," Tyler said. "What are you still doing at the station? Where's the night dispatcher?"

"His kid's got a soccer match. I told him I'd fill in till he could get here. Do you want to know why I called?"

Flicking an apologetic gaze at Andrea, he leaned next to her against the sofa. "Why not?"

"Sister Mary Katherine needs you at the church."

"Now? I haven't broken any commandments."

Andrea commanded the guilty flush rising up her cheeks to chill. Mention of the sister certainly wasn't conducive to sizzling romance.

"Can't it wait?" Tyler added to Aqua.

"'Fraid not," Aqua said. "The chalice is missing."

The sizzle froze in its tracks.

"The chalice?" Tyler repeated incredulously, even as Andrea silently mouthed the same words.

"You know," Aqua continued, "the cup the priest uses for communion. Apparently, it's pretty valuable. And historic. Not to mention, well, sacred. I'm thinking you should get right over there."

Tyler closed his eyes. "Please tell me it's not silver."

"You're doomed to disappointment, boss."

DESPITE TYLER'S BEST efforts, shaking Andrea proved impossible.

He wanted her around, of course. Always, in fact. Just

not during a police investigation in which her brother was the prime suspect.

Hell, the *only* suspect.

"It's unconscionable," Father Dominick said for at least the fifth time.

"Yes, sir," Tyler said, trying to remain calm while Sister Mary Katherine sat stiffly in the front pew and Andrea paced in front of the altar.

The time for Dwayne gathering evidence had passed, so Tyler had called the county crime lab, and two of their techs had already arrived and were in the storage closet off the vestibule where the chalice was kept, dusting for prints and other evidence. The padlock had been busted with a heavy object, but, otherwise, Tyler hadn't observed anything else out of the ordinary.

No one he'd questioned so far had seen any unusual cars in the parking lot that day. No one had seen anyone entering the sanctuary.

Of course, there were a couple of people he'd yet to talk to, namely the head custodian, who worked only during the day, and recently hired church errand boy, Finn Hastings. Tyler wanted to hear preliminary results from the techs before going forward, which was why he'd wound up listening to Father Dominick's laments in the meantime.

"The cup dates back to the late 1700s," the priest went on, wringing his hands. "It's part of island history. Not to mention priceless."

Tyler wished with everything in him that he'd never hear those two sentences again. But if he didn't get a handle on these thefts, priceless history would succinctly describe his law enforcement career.

His very brief career.

"Who could possibly be so desperate as to steal from the church?" Father Dominick asked to the room at large. "Our parishioners are generous. Our community is close-knit. We help everyone who comes to us."

"The desperate don't always ask for help," Sister Mary Katherine said, who'd amazingly picked up a wad of white knitting and starting clicking her needles.

Father Dominick appeared not to hear her. "Other items are missing as well, so I read in the newspaper. What progress has been made, Deputy?"

"Some. We've questioned several people. Unfortunately, there isn't much to go on at the moment."

"Tyler is spending every waking minute working on the case," Andrea added, sounding distracted as she paced.

"I appreciate your confidence in him," Father Dominick said, "but I'm afraid the situation has reached a crisis. Henrietta Jackson is running on about some silly alien story, but I'm sure everyone will agree that the thief is very human and escalating in his or her crimes."

"That's true, Father," Tyler said, taking the criticism with a nod. "Please remember these thefts have taken place in less than a week. The sheriff's department is doing all it can."

"I'm sure it is," the priest said, obviously trying to be kind. "But when is Sheriff Caldwell due back from his vacation?"

"Next Sunday," Tyler answered.

Father Dominick nodded gravely. "Perhaps the time has come for him to return early."

Andrea's expression was thunderous. "Hel—"

"Andrea," Sister Mary Katherine broke in as she stood. "I'm sure you don't want to finish that."

Andrea crossed her arms over her chest. "Sure I do."

The sister's gaze didn't budge. "But you shouldn't."

Finally, Andrea nodded. "Yes, ma'am."

The whole situation was too intense, too personal. Tyler had been removed in many ways from his military missions. They'd been ordered for one, and decisions to move or not move had been made way above his rank. With precise training, he'd done his job and nearly always succeeded.

Facing victims and the unknown was much harder, and he'd garnered a new level of respect for Sheriff Caldwell in the last few days. And that man, revered by everyone, had left *him* to handle things while he was gone. Considering how particular and picky the sheriff was, the confidence of that single gesture should be enough to get Tyler through this mess.

Besides, he had Andrea.

She thought he was the best, even when he wasn't. He was incredibly grateful to have her on his side, even though he feared she wouldn't be able to stand with him much longer. Her brother was part of the investigation, and now a theft had taken place mere yards from his apartment. Beyond that, Tyler had secrets he wouldn't, *couldn't* reveal, or risk losing her forever.

To say things didn't look good for him or the ex-con was a ridiculous understatement.

So, even though he didn't want to insult the clergy present, it was Andrea he was concerned about.

Crossing to her, he grasped both her hands in his. "I've got this," he said quietly.

Her sea-green eyes fired with temper. "I know." Her gaze shot to Father Dominick. "I seem to be the only one who thinks so, however."

"It's tense for everybody."

"You have any theories?"

"None that make sense. Stealing from a church is a whole different element."

Her gaze dropped briefly. "It's a little scary."

With every cell in his body, he was suppressing his anger. Fury led nowhere productive. As he knew all too well. "I'll find the answers."

"Sure you will. But—" She searched his gaze. "You're awfully calm."

"That's my job." He managed a half smile. "Well, hopefully."

"It will be," she assured him, and hugged him briefly.

He was encouraged by the public show of affection. Maybe she wouldn't dump him after he questioned her brother. Again.

"I'm going to see Finn."

Wincing, Tyler held on to her hands. "You can't."

"Sure I can." She nodded toward the door leading to the church grounds. "His apartment is right there, over the building used for storage and events."

"I know, but I have to see his reaction to news of the theft. You can't warn him I'm here."

As the full meaning of his words hit her, her gaze drilled into his. "You're not calm. You're made of ice."

Accepting the dart, he nodded. "I'm sorry."

Without another word, she turned away from him.

Tyler shoved his hands in the pockets of his pants. "That went well."

"Deputy." One of the crime scene techs approached. "I'm CSI Mike Stearns. I think you ought to see this."

With Andrea tagging behind, Stearns led Tyler through

the sanctuary and across the vestibule to a small side door where another tech had knelt on the carpeted floor.

A clear print of a muddy shoe was visible.

"The trail gets lighter," Stearns said, pointing at the trail, "but it leads right to the storage closet."

"Looks like a work boot," the tech kneeling on the front said.

"There's a custodian," Tyler said.

Stearns shrugged. "Probably belongs to him. We'll get measurements and pictures and make a cast. You never know."

With all the bad news he'd gotten in the last few hours, Tyler clung to the slight hope that the case could be solved over a rainstorm and a bad guy with distinctive footwear.

"Finn wears tennis shoes," Andrea said from behind him.

Loyal to a fault. It was one of her finest qualities.

He admired so much about her—her passion and her quick mind especially. He was damn tired of some unknown guy with sticky hands getting between them.

Last night during his confrontation with Finn, he'd reflected that he wanted to make her happy more than he wanted to solve the case, but now he knew neither of them could be happy, or truly be together, until the thefts were closed.

And he wanted to be with her like he wanted to breathe.

She'd come to mean so much to him so quickly, and yet it also seemed like he'd spent his life searching for her, walking a path that would lead back to the island he loved, and the woman he was meant to find.

"We've also got some fibers and lots of prints," Stearns said.

Tyler sighed. "How many of those belong to the priest, nuns or altar boys?"

Stearns, who had seen-and-done-it-all eyes, shrugged again. "Quite a few, I'd guess. We'll know more in a few days."

"Thanks." He handed Stearns a card with his office, home and cell numbers on it. "I appreciate you guys coming out."

"We've got the prints you sent over from the other thefts, so we'll let you know if we find any matches."

"You'll compare them to the criminal database?"

Stearns nodded. "Sure. That's standard op."

Tyler couldn't imagine direct, no-bull Finn skulking around the church and helping himself to a priceless and holy relic, but he had to be eliminated definitively as a suspect. And he had to be questioned.

"I'm going to talk to Finn."

She stomped toward the front door. "Try to stop me from coming with you, and I'm calling his lawyer. You won't come near him until sometime in the next century."

"I'm not going to stop you. I'd like you to be there, in fact."

She opened the door and stalked off across the lawn. "Fine."

"I still want you," he said, catching up to her.

"You're an ass."

"I'm a cop. And I still want you."

Her long, angry strides made quick progress toward the brick-and-stone building where her brother's apartment was located. "I want you, too. But I really don't like you very much."

Well, he'd always enjoyed a good challenge. "At this point, I'm willing to take what I can get."

10

"THIS IS GETTING TO be a habit, Deputy," Finn said when he opened his apartment door.

Remembering she'd said those same words, Andrea nearly smiled. But the guarded, tense look on her brother's face stopped her.

"I'd like to talk to you," Tyler said.

Andrea moved past him and embraced Finn. "You've been here all night, haven't you?"

"Andrea…" Tyler began in warning.

She ignored her lover and hooked her hand around Finn's arm. "Let's sit."

There wasn't much room for conversation. A double-size bed on a wooden frame, a cushy navy-blue chair and matching ottoman, a dresser and a TV on a stand pretty much summed up the sparse furnishings. She knew Finn had proudly earned the money to buy each and every piece.

He wouldn't go back to stealing. He simply wouldn't.

"What's missing now?" Finn asked on a tired sigh as he lowered himself next to Andrea on the bed.

Tyler chose to stand—the position of authority and intimidation. "Give me a rundown of your schedule today."

After a questioning glance at Andrea, which she answered with a nod, he ran through getting up and meeting the sisters and Father Dominick for breakfast in the rectory, then going through his assigned errands, including a trip to the hardware store and delivering two meals to elderly church members.

His voice was calm and controlled. Andrea was sure that she, who knew him so well, was the only one who noticed the nerves underneath.

"Did you go into the sanctuary?" Tyler asked, his blue eyes carefully blank.

Andrea squeezed Finn's hand, silently offering support, as well as hoping he'd be both brief and honest.

"No," Finn said firmly.

"You didn't pass through there, maybe to ask the priest a question or to take a shortcut to the rectory?"

"No."

"Have you ever been in the storage closet off the vestibule?"

The abrupt shift made Finn pause before answering. "Sure," he said with a shrug. "Lots of times. The communion sacraments are—"

Andrea squeezed his hand hard to stop him. Should she have called Carr?

Tyler never looked her way, but he shifted his tactics. "If you've been in the closet," he said to Finn, "you must know its contents. Describe the items kept there."

"The sacraments—you know, the bread and wine, plus the communion cup, trays, offering plates, candles and acolyte lighters."

"If you need to get something from the closet, how do you get in? There's a padlock."

"I have a key."

Surprise flickered through Tyler's eyes. "A key?"

"Sure." He reached across Andrea and grabbed a ring of keys off the bedside table. "I have a key to everything except private offices."

Relief flooded Andrea. Sister Mary Katherine and Father Dominick trusted Finn just as she did. "Well, I'd say that was a big, fat mistake on the thief's part."

Tyler's gaze met hers. The hardness in his eyes faltered for a moment before he directed his attention to her brother. "Have you unlocked the cabinet for anybody today?"

Andrea jumped off the bed, incensed by the trickery. "Hang on, Lieutenant. The lock was "

"Sit down, Andrea," Tyler ordered. "Or you're out."

So much for working together.

With a silent glare, she did as requested.

"Finn—the closet," Tyler prompted. "Did you open it for yourself or anyone else today?"

"No."

"Did you see anyone near the closet today?"

"No. I never went in the sanctuary. What's missing?"

Tyler simply shook his head. "Have you seen anybody lurking around the church grounds in the last few days?"

"Lurking, sir?"

"You know what I mean—casing."

Finn looked amused. "I don't really know much about casing, sir. I pretty much stole on impulse."

"You're definitely related to Andrea," Tyler muttered.

"You'd know him better if you talked to him instead of interrogating him," Andrea said sweetly.

Clearly frustrated, Tyler scanned the room—which didn't take long. "The chalice is missing," he said after a minute.

Finn lurched to his feet. "I didn't take it." His hazel eyes were full of panic. "I wouldn't do that to the church, or Sister Mary Katherine."

Rising, Andrea grabbed his hand. "We know you didn't. Don't we, Lieutenant?"

Tyler slid his hands in his uniform pockets, his gaze locking with hers.

Andrea understood his silence. If he agreed, he was breaking probably a hundred rules of law enforcement and, at least in his mind, possibly jeopardizing his case.

But his answer was a vital test to her. Were they building a relationship or just sleeping together? Could she truly believe in the passion he seemed to have for her? Maybe she didn't have the right to ask for his trust, but she wanted it anyway.

"I don't think you're the thief, Finn," Tyler said finally.

So maybe she *did* like him. A lot.

Closing the two feet that separated them, she wrapped her arms around his neck and kissed him. A gasp escaped his lips before he responded.

"See, I'm not such a bad guy," Tyler said when she pulled away, his gaze fixed on hers.

Andrea knew she could look into those bright eyes for a long, long time and never tire of the desire she found in them. And those feelings scared her. How much further could she fall?

"You're okay," she said lightly, belying the concern in her heart.

Grinning, Tyler raised his eyebrows. "I'll work on improving."

"Are you guys done with me?" Finn asked from behind them. "This is kinda awkward."

His expression sobering, Tyler stepped away from Andrea. "I'm finished, but I'm sure you'll be hearing from me." When Andrea cast him a questioning glance, he added, "I don't think Finn's involved, but somebody is stealing silver on the island. And they're doing a pretty damn good job making him look guilty."

Andrea frowned. "Then doesn't the thief have to be somebody Finn knows?"

"Maybe not," Tyler said with a shrug. "It's a small island. A lot of people probably know about his past trouble with the law. And with everything he does here at the church, a lot more know about his job."

A thief with a grudge? Andrea shook her head in denial. "But why would anybody do that? Who would hate him so much?"

Finn hunched his shoulders. "Ex-con in town. Easy blame."

The cynicism in his tone made Andrea's stomach tighten.

To her surprise, Tyler nodded. "Finn's a convenient scapegoat. I don't think it's about hate, though. Probably not a personal thing." His gaze shifted to Finn. "But just in case, I want the names of the gang members you used to hang out with."

Finn lowered his head. "Ah, man. I left all that behind."

"Some mistakes you never stop paying for," Tyler returned, his voice firm.

Like the mistakes he'd made? She was really getting aggravated by his cryptic hints. He didn't want to talk to her about it, but he kept bringing it up? What was his deal?

"How encouraging," she said.

"But true," Tyler insisted. "If we're going to solve this case, we've got to be honest with each other."

With a knowing stare, she crossed her arms over her chest. "Do we really?"

"Andy," Finn said, saving Tyler from a reply, "it's cool." He shrugged. "He's right. I'd rather hear it straight."

Andrea never budged her stare from Tyler. "So would I."

Tyler—the big chicken—shifted his gaze to her brother. "Finn, I need you to think back over the last few weeks. Has anybody been acting unusual, asking questions about your past, your schedule?"

"I don't think so," Finn said.

"Well, think harder," Tyler suggested. "The election is in less than two weeks."

"And may justice be done regardless," Andrea added.

Finn glanced up. "Yeah, sure."

Andrea pulled him into a hug. "We *will* find the truth."

Finn stepped back from her embrace. "I know."

Since he didn't sound so sure, she held his hand a moment longer. "You're not alone. Not anymore."

"But I'd like to be." Finn squeezed her hand, then let go. "No offense."

She wasn't. In his place, she'd want some time on her own. Besides, she had issues to discuss with Tyler. "Fine. We'll go."

As they left the building and headed toward Tyler's squad car, neither of them spoke. Absently noting the thickness of the night sky and the crisp breeze, signaling an approaching storm, Andrea organized her thoughts. She needed to get to the bottom of this *I've killed* business.

Even though there were a million things to do in order to solve the silver thefts, she couldn't let his obvious pain go on any longer. He blamed himself, and since her journey with Finn had filled her with the same emotion many times over, she knew how lousy it felt.

Tyler opened her door, then climbed in the driver's side of the gold-and-blue sheriff's department car. As he gripped the steering wheel, his gaze fixated on the church, lit by spotlights surrounded by a group of ancient oaks. "It's been a really stressful day."

Just like that, her conversation plan crashed. The tension in his body, the bleakness in his eyes, said plenty on their own. The issues she wanted to address could wait.

Now, she only wanted his touch and knew he needed hers. She slid her hand along his thigh. "I bet I can find a way to relieve that stress."

Dragging his gaze away from the church, he took her hand, kissing the spot on the underside of her wrist where her pulse beat thick and strong. "Please do."

A sensual smile breaking across her lips, she unhooked her seat belt and moved into his lap. With one hand still on his thigh, she glided the other one up his chest and pressed her mouth to the side of his neck.

"You're breaking several laws, you know."

"You want to ticket me?" she asked, then flicked her tongue against his ear.

He sucked in a quick breath. "Not really."

"Then drive."

Though he groaned, he put the car in Reverse. "I don't see how."

She threaded her fingers in the thick, silky hair at his nape and let her lips roam across his cheek, then down his throat. The scent of arousal, the sound of labored breathing and glorious, enticing heat filled the cab. Yanking his shirt from his pants and flipping open the top button, she glided her palm down his body.

The car swerved.

She smiled.

With the speed limit on the island a sedate thirty-five and her confidence in Tyler's reflexes, she sank her teeth lightly into his earlobe as she wrapped her hand around his erection.

He braked hard.

"In a minute, you'll have to arrest yourself," she said.

"In a minute, I'm—"

He stopped talking as she moved her hand briskly up, then down. His cock pulsed, and she felt the echo between her own legs. When she scooted over the console and replaced her mouth with her hand, he yanked the car to the shoulder of the road.

"Dear heaven," he whispered thickly, throwing the gear into Park.

As his hands tangled in her hair, she moved over him, deciding his tension had flown completely...except for one particular area.

She liked having him under her complete control; she liked knowing everything they shared strengthened their bond. She loved touching him and relished his touch in return. Whatever became of them, however long they lasted, she hoped she'd never regret taking this chance.

"I've never had sex in a police car," she said, lifting her head and swinging her legs over to straddle his hips.

His eyes glittered in the dim light. "Hell, the car's not mine. It's the sheriff's. How am I going to—"

She silenced him by kissing him full on the mouth. Gliding her tongue across his, she moaned in the back of her throat at the intimate but ultimately frustrating contact between her sundress, panties and his erection.

"Do you want me?" she asked, closing her eyes as he pressed his hips harder against hers and her breath hitched.

"Always."

"Then get me home."

"My place is closer." Working his arms around her, while she plastered herself to his chest and tried to calm her racing heart, he threw the car in gear and flew the remaining distance to his house. The tires squealed as he whipped the car into his driveway. Barely before the car had stopped, he'd opened her door and was waiting.

They linked hands and rushed inside a small white cottage. She had a glimpse of a den to the right and a short hall leading to a bedroom on the left, then he led her straight down the hall into his kitchen.

It was neat and smelled of spaghetti sauce, the bachelor's steady meal. Someone, probably Tyler's mother, had put a blue glass vase filled with tropical silk flowers on the kitchen table.

Tyler snagged the vase and set it on the kitchen counter, then lifted her onto the table.

"No tour?" she teased.

"Later." He tossed his keys aside, then kissed her until she forgot where she was, much less why she'd care to know.

He freed his erection as she wriggled out of her undies, then kicked them aside. He grabbed a condom from his wallet, and she helped him roll on the protection with frantic speed. With his arms braced around her, she hooked her legs around his hips. "Have I told you lately how much I love that you love to wear dresses?"

"Ah…no. Not lately."

"Then I'll say it now." He surged inside her.

She absorbed the stabbing pleasure and clung to him. Her heart warned her that the echoes of their pleasure would resonate through her life, possibly forever. Their time together was precious, sweeping them along like the ocean clutched at the sand, dragging bits and pieces, swirling where some returned to the shore and others sunk to the blackened bottom, lost without light.

His hips pounded against hers, and she lost the power of breath and thought. The intense pleasure spiraled and tightened until she exploded, throbbing over him, clinging to his body, wondering if she'd ever reach his heart or let hers be fully his.

He followed her climax a heartbeat later, and her body trembled, even as her soul sighed with satisfaction and her legs slid weakly off his hips.

LIFTING HER HEAD OFF the pillow briefly, Andrea pressed an exhausted but satisfied kiss to Tyler's bare chest.

After the intensity of their stress-busting sex on the kitchen table, he'd said little, simply leading her to his bedroom, where his hunger continued at an almost desperate pace. She knew the anxiety of the thefts, the election, as well as his mysterious mistake, were fueling a drive to escape. And while she was only too happy to sail off to Neverland with him, the journey would inevitably manage to find ground at some point.

She hoped his touchdown wouldn't be part of an emergency crash landing.

"Will your contacts let you know if they hear anything more about the tea set?" he asked, his eyes still closed.

"They will," she said, fighting to shift her thoughts from lovemaking to law enforcement.

He moved them onto their sides, legs tangled, sharing the same pillow. "What do you think we're up against?"

"I think the timing and the election are significant. I

wonder if the theft of the chalice was simply to throw suspicion on Finn, and I still don't understand why anything was stolen. What's the thief really after? What's really at stake here?"

In the dim light of the moon shining through the bedroom window, his intense daze searched hers. "A great deal."

Did he mean them or the case? Or both?

"You were great tonight," he added. "Defending me to a priest and a nun."

"You believe my brother's innocent."

"I do," he said, cupping her cheek in his hand. "You defended me before that."

"I believe in you."

"Because I was your high school crush?"

"Because of much more."

"What then?" he asked, his voice soft.

She wished she could be more eloquent, find the words that would make all the turbulence in his eyes grow calm. She wished she could trust in her feelings. "You're special."

She'd said the wrong thing. With a sigh, he sat up and flung the covers aside, then snatched his uniform pants from the floor. "So I've been told all my life," he said as he dressed.

"Why's that bad?" she asked reasonably, tucking the sheet around her and propping her head on her hand.

He paused a telling moment before saying, "It's not."

Family and duty. She had to find a way to get to that kernel. "Your grandfather was sheriff, right?"

He clenched his fists at his sides, so she knew she was on the right track.

"He was."

"I don't really remember before Sheriff Caldwell, but I've heard your grandfather was well respected."

"I remember," he said heatedly. "And if I forget, there's a scrapbook."

Her own parents and grandparents were gone, but she understood this kind of pressure easily. She and Finn were the only ones left to insure their generation did right by their name. "So your family expects you to win this election."

"Yes."

"Do you want to win?"

"I…" He was obviously surprised by the direct question. "Sure I do."

"That didn't sound so decisive."

"I'm sure."

"I can see that."

"No, I don't think you can."

"And why do you think that is?"

He crossed his arms over his chest. "You're wrapped up too intimately in this case."

"Well, that's certainly true, but I'm not worried about Finn any longer. I'm worried about you."

"You shouldn't be." He made a visible effort to rein in his emotions and sat beside her on the edge of the bed. "I'm handling it."

Despite his efforts, despair rolled off him like the waves battering the sandy shore. He hid his pain behind a hero's reputation and a flirtatious smile. "You're not handling anything."

11

Faced with those all-knowing sea-green eyes, Tyler fought to deny the turmoil churning in his gut.

She made him feel good. Amazing, even. He didn't want the past jumping in to spoil their bond.

"You know you can tell me anything," she said.

"Yes."

"But…"

"No but."

She sat up, sliding the back of her hand across his cheek. The tender gesture made his throat close. "Why did you retire?"

You're not alone, not anymore.

She'd said those words to her brother. The fact that she was willing to stand up for him as well overwhelmed him. All those years ago, he hadn't seen her, but his focus was clear now. She was loyal and strong, beautiful and compassionate, challenging and brilliant.

It was ridiculously obvious that he loved her.

She was everything he needed to make his life complete. She was what had been missing from his supposedly perfect life. He'd risk or do anything to have her by his side.

With feelings of that depth running through his veins,

he had no right to keep secrets, to hold back the worst of him. If he ever hoped to have her love and respect in return, she had to know the truth.

Even if he risked everything.

He rose and held out his hand. "Let's go into the den."

After helping her dress in his uniform shirt, which looked a hell of a lot better on her anyway, he got them some orange juice from the kitchen, then sat beside her on his rented brown leatherette couch.

If he was going to win Andrea's heart, he'd have to get over his commitment issues and actually buy some decent furniture.

"I was called in the middle of the night to head a mission in…" He paused, considering security clearances, information he'd sworn to protect, along with lives. "Terrorists had taken over a village, and we'd been quietly asked to assist in apprehending the suspects and turning them over to local military."

"Quietly?"

"It's not the sort of thing you'd see on the news unless the mission went horribly wrong."

"Which, I'm guessing, it did."

His heart lurched as he recalled the noisy firefight, the panic and screams amid a cloud of dust. "The terrorists were bigger in numbers and better armed than I anticipated. Three guys on my team were killed."

"By the terrorists?"

"Yes, but my aggressive tactics caused them to be in the vulnerable position in the first place. I should have done more recon. I should have anticipated the ambush."

"I would think their job made them vulnerable."

Her blind defense suddenly made him angry, though he

knew from intimate experience that fury led nowhere. "I screwed up!"

"So why didn't you die?" she asked softly.

"I have no idea."

"I'm assuming you weren't the only one who escaped."

"Nine out of twelve." He bowed his head, gripping his juice until he was sure it would shatter in his hands. "The military considered the mission a success."

"You don't, of course." She drew her hand up his back. "And you maybe shouldn't. You made a mistake, but since you were trying to save innocent people at the time, the government—and any other sane individual—should give you a break. Did your commander force you to retire?"

"He offered a leave of absence, time to get my head together and get counseling. I refused." He lifted his shoulders to try to shrug off the decision he'd come to, but he knew he wasn't doing nonchalance very well. "I can't be trusted with other people's lives anymore."

"Which is why you're scared of becoming sheriff."

He cast her a surprised glance. How did she always understand so easily? Was he that transparent, or was she that intuitive?

"These are the most important people in your life —your family, friends, people you grew up with. You don't want to risk them."

He'd add her, and even Finn, to that list, but he didn't want to distract her. "What if I screw up again?"

"News flash, Mr. Wanna-be Sheriff, you *are* going to screw up again. You're not perfect, and nobody expects you to be."

"My family—"

"Will love you no matter what. Do they know about the failed mission?" When he shook his head, she added, "You need to tell them."

"But I was the quarterback, student class president, Most Likely to Succeed, Most Popular, honor graduate, war hero. All those accomplishments are listed on my election posters. I'm a fraud. I'm none of those things."

"Mr. Everything has flaws. Well, ain't that a kick in the pants?"

He scowled. "You're making me feel foolish."

"I'm sorry. You're not." She set the juice glasses on the coffee table and linked their hands. "And you still are all those things. It's the way you deal with your setbacks that make you amazing, not having them in the first place." She searched his gaze, her bright eyes glittering. "What if I'd given up on being with you?" she asked.

"But you didn't. You went after what you wanted."

She smiled. "With a little pushing and shoving by a friend, yeah. You need to put what's happened to you into perspective. If guilt keeps you from being sheriff, then the loss you've suffered will only become greater."

The heaviness in his chest suddenly lightened, and he pulled her into his arms, holding her in exactly the place he wanted her to stay forever. She sighed and hugged him tight.

It was crazy…her not turning away from him. He could hardly believe he'd shared something so intimate with a woman he was seeing. He'd never trusted anyone to that extent.

But when the unexpected jumped from behind a dark corner, Andrea was the one who'd have his back.

She didn't seem at all phased by his terrible revelations. She loved and accepted her brother, even with the mistakes he'd made, so Tyler should have realized that telling her the truth wouldn't be so hard. And despite the fact that they had to solve this case and clear Finn, plus get himself elected, none of that seemed like a burden, or even so difficult anymore.

The understanding in her eyes had given him back the hope he'd lost.

"Do you want to withdraw from the election?" she asked, leaning back to meet his gaze.

"And leave Lester Cradock in charge of law and order? Hell, no."

"Really? I was so looking forward to finding the next cutting-edge belt designer who could accommodate bull-whip attachments."

"Indiana Jones has long-cornered the market anyway."

"Unfortunate for Lester, but probably true."

He laid his hand against her cheek. "You're pretty amazing."

Rising, she wrapped her hand around his wrist and tugged him down the hall to his bedroom. "Am I? I bet I can upgrade that assessment."

She offered her support and her body, but he knew he hadn't yet reached her heart. Since he'd only realized his own feelings not long ago, he'd have to be patient, let their connection grow and build until she, too, realized they were meant to be together.

And in the meantime, he intended to catch a thief.

THE NEXT MORNING, TYLER walked up the stairs to the sheriff's department with a genuine attitude of optimism and promise.

Through the thefts and election preparation, he'd been

moving forward with half his heart. Until last night, he hadn't felt worthy of walking in either Sheriff Caldwell's or his grandfather's shoes.

And though he'd never forget the mistakes he'd made and the lives lost as a result, he was confident he could do the job the islanders would—hopefully—entrust to him.

Inside, Aqua wasn't at her desk, but the object of Dwayne's undying devotion, Misty Mickerson, and her three-year-old son, Jack, sat in the waiting room. "Can we talk?" she asked, standing and tucking a strand of her bright red hair behind her ear.

Clutching his toy plastic police car in his chubby hand, Jack, his white-blond locks a stark contrast to his mother's, gave Tyler a broad grin.

"Your ex?" Tyler asked Misty, wondering how they could have that kind of conversation in front of Jack.

"No. I haven't heard from him in months. This is about Dwayne."

Tyler was even more confused, but he nodded. "Come on back." Still wondering where Aqua had gotten off to, he led Misty and Jack to the sheriff's office.

There, Misty laid down a blanket for the toddler and surrounded him with a collection of toys before she sat in the visitor's chair in front of the desk. "He'll be happy," she said, casting her son a tired but proud glance. "For a good ten minutes anyway."

"What's up?" Tyler asked, leaning against the desk.

"You know Dwayne pretty well, right?"

"I guess." Explaining about his tendency to hyperventilate probably wasn't something Misty needed to know. "We work together every day. He's a good cop...a reliable, thorough man." He flicked his gaze to Jack and wondered if he might be pushing it when he added, "He'd make a good father someday."

Misty sighed. "I want Dwayne to make a move."

"A—" Tyler stopped. From what he'd heard, all Dwayne did was make moves. None of which had been reciprocated. "Pardon me?"

"He's been asking me out nearly every week for the last two years. But, lately, nothing. He says he's busy—working with you on a case."

The accusation in her tone was unmistakable.

Hang on. "Why didn't you accept one of his offers before now?"

She shrugged. "I just liked him asking."

And people thought Tyler was a ladies' man. He'd never understand the gender if he made decoding them his life's work. To think he'd been in a good mood less than ten minutes ago. "If you're just going to turn him down again, why should I convince him to ask you out?"

"I'm ready to accept now."

"Why?"

Her soft brown eyes twinkled. "He's a good cop, a reliable, thorough man. He'd make a good father someday."

"Uh-huh. A hundred or so dinner invitations, and zippo. But on my recommendation, you're willing to give him a chance."

"Yes."

"Why?"

"You and the sheriff said almost the identical thing about him. So I figure I'd been holding out a little *too* long. I mean, after my ex's drunken tantrums, I had a right to be cautious, but the most potent thing Dwayne drinks is coffee at Mabel's, and he's so quiet and gentle. Maybe it's time I move on."

"The sheriff?" Tyler repeated. Those were the only words he'd really heard. "When did you talk to the sheriff?"

"About ten minutes before you came in. He left with the receptionist—the one with blue streaks in her hair. I'm sure they'll be back—"

"But he's in Bermuda."

"Not anymore."

Tyler's heart jumped. "You're saying Sheriff Buddy Caldwell—big guy, Stetson hat, boots—he's on the island?" He pointed at the scuffed wooden floor. "*This* island."

"Sure. I guess he was on vacation or something, but—" She stopped as Tyler straightened abruptly. "What?"

"He wasn't due back until next Sunday."

"Oh, well. I guess he changed his plans."

He'd been in a *really* good mood ten minutes ago.

While Tyler's mind was racing about which victim— Mrs. Jackson, Cal Wells or the Catholic Church—might have called him home, the imposing figure of the man himself filled the doorway.

Nodding briefly at Misty, he crossed his arms over his massive chest. Then he transferred his gaze to Tyler, who could have sworn the other man's piercing blue eyes bored a hole through his skull. "I hear your big case is headed for the crapper."

12

"LET'S GO BACK TO THE people who had contact with Mrs. Jackson," the sheriff said. "Do any of them cross-reference with friends or associates of Cal Jones or the church leaders?"

While the sheriff sat behind his desk, Tyler was wearing out the floor. "It might be easier to count people who don't. More than half the people on the island attend St. Matthews."

Rubbing his stubble-laden jaw, Sheriff Caldwell nodded. "True. We have a devout population."

"And one bad egg."

Again, the sheriff nodded. A man of few words.

With all his intimidating bluster, his boss and mentor had been really cool about the theft case. Though he'd come back from vacation early, he'd blamed the decision on too much sun and lousy fishing. Tyler was positive he was lying, but other than his opening dig, he hadn't shown a moment of regret that he'd recommended Tyler for his job or disappointment in the way he'd handled the investigation so far.

"No leads from the pawnshops?" the sheriff asked.

"None. The stolen items haven't shown up anywhere."

"At least none you've been told about."

The phone rang, interrupting Tyler's reply. The calls came every few minutes—from city council members, concerned citizens, the mayor. They were never going to get the case solved if they were picking up the phone and calming everybody's nerves every five minutes.

"The mayor again," the sheriff said shortly as he hung up the phone.

"Maybe we'll hear something later today from the faxes and e-mail alerts we sent out this morning," Tyler said, getting back to the case details.

"I'm havin' a hard time picturin' the tea set or chalice turning up in the average pawnshop."

"I have some unusual outlets covered, too." As he'd sent messages to pawnshops, he'd also e-mailed Andrea to ask her to check in with her "friends."

The sheriff raised his bushy eyebrows. "Such as?"

"A friend who's a fraud specialist is checking with some of her acquaintances. They're in the professional acquisitions industry, so they might have a lead."

"Thieves, in other words."

"Well…yes, sir."

"And you don't suspect this friend's acquaintances in our case?"

"No, sir. I get the feeling we're too small-time for them."

"If the Hope diamond goes missing…"

"They'd be the first ones to call. But, thankfully, that wouldn't be our jurisdiction."

"True." The sheriff leaned back in his chair. "But maybe there is a ring of thieves at work. A small-time one. There's a lot of money on the island. Maybe they figure it's a nice, quiet place to set up shop."

"Could be, I guess," Tyler said respectfully, even though he didn't think that was the case. "They haven't stolen much for a group."

"They're at three, and we got zip. I'd say they aren't havin' any trouble scoring."

Tyler felt his face heat. "Good point."

"We'll catch up, Deputy. This community's strong. We'll pull together and find this creep. Or creeps."

On that note, the phone rang again. Tyler tried to remember the support and understanding he'd seen in Andrea's eyes the night before.

He needed her solace even more now.

ANDREA POLISHED OFF THE last of her cinnamon crumb cake and silently praised the mixture of butter, eggs, sugar and flour in the hands of a bakery master.

Maybe Gilda's Gourmet Delights, with its confectionary bright-pink-and-silver decor, was an odd place for the discussion of a task force, but this was Palmer's Island, after all.

"Are you sure they're okay with this?" Andrea asked Sloan for what had to be the twentieth time.

"Stop worrying," Sloan said, checking her makeup from a compact she'd pulled out of her purse. "Men always appreciate help." She paused significantly. "As long as it's accompanied by a good bribe."

Andrea glanced across the table, meeting Sister Mary Katherine's gaze.

"It's fine," the nun said reassuringly. "I can usually get Father Dominick to see my point more clearly when I bring a tin of cookies to the meeting."

It was an odd task force—the fourth member of which was waiting at the police station—but Andrea was confident they could make a difference in solving the silver case.

She wasn't, however, quite so sure the sheriff and his deputies would see things that way. Which was why they'd stopped by Gilda's to strategize over coffee and cake, and, of course, bring the men a tasty bribe in their effort to persuade them they needed help on the case.

What lawman doesn't crave peach pie after a long, hard day catching bad guys?

And if she felt silly about the strategy, she only had to glance at Sloan to know what she'd say.

"We've got to get you out of the insurance business," she said. "It's made you a worrier."

"I've always been a worrier."

Sloan shrugged even as her blue eyes gleamed. "I'll handle everything."

Somehow, Andrea wasn't convinced.

They gathered their bags and the pie, waved goodbye to Gilda, then headed across the street to city hall, where Andrea's concerns were realized. "Great," she muttered, recognizing the beady eyes and moplike hair of the man loitering on the steps with another sleazy-looking guy. "The press has arrived."

Flipping her hair over her shoulder, Sloan snorted. "Some press. Jerry Mescle and his cousin Clyde."

"Oh, my," Sister Mary Katherine said. "That poor boy always did make unfortunate choices in apparel."

As Andrea climbed from the car, she studied the men and presumed the sister was referring to Clyde, who was wearing a white T-shirt with dirt-brown polyester pants.

"Is there a Patron Saint of Polyester, Sister?" Sloan asked as they started up the stone stairs.

She shook her head. "I always defer to Jude in these situations."

"Lost causes," Andrea said. "Appropriate."

The two men rushed them, Jerry shoving a tape recorder

in Andrea's face and Clyde holding up his cell phone, presumably to take a picture. "What do you know about the maniac on the loose on our island?" Jerry shouted.

"I'm ready to call a cop," Sloan said, shifting her stiletto sandal dangerously close to Jerry's beat-up tennis shoes. "Especially since the maniac's standing right in front of me."

"Don't you feel that law enforcement has aggressively failed us in—"

"I think you need to take a giant step backward," Andrea warned, shifting her body in front of Sister Mary Katherine. "We're here on a spiritual mission."

"Sister." Jerry pushed the tape recorder over Andrea's shoulder. "How do you feel about the missing chalice? Are you here to take the sheriff and his incompetent staff to task for their failure of civic duty?"

Sister Mary Katherine's voice was scalding. "I'm here, young man, to bring peach pie to our hardworking civil servants."

Jerry obviously wanted to say more, but the sister in her traditional habit was a pretty intimidating sight, so he stepped aside.

"Can I go back and stomp him?" Sloan asked as they made their way to the door.

"Later," Andrea muttered. "Let's not cause a bigger scene. Anything we do or say will wind up in the paper."

"With Jerry's personal spin." Sloan nodded. "I get it. The election is twelve days away."

Once they were inside, the waiting area was deserted. Aqua, who completed their double-X-chromosome task force, waved to them from her glassed-in office. "Are they busy?" Andrea asked.

Aqua rolled her black-rimmed eyes. "Still yammering. I thought lawmen were supposed to be the strong, silent type. But those dudes can *talk*."

As she rose—barefoot—to lead them back to the sheriff's office, Andrea noticed both her fingernails and toes were painted a shade of electric-green. With her long, multicolored bohemian skirt and skimpy white tank, which revealed a dangling belly-button ring, she wasn't the average person's idea of a police dispatcher, but Andrea admired her funky, uninhibited style.

Andrea's own wardrobe seemed boring by comparison. Like the night of the costume ball, she felt the unfamiliar call of daring. She'd been responsible and conservative her whole life. It had led to plenty of professional success, but not so much in the personal arena.

Giving in to boldness had led to a relationship with Tyler. With him, she was pretending to be the woman she'd longed to turn into. If she continued on that road, would she be adventurous permanently? Would forbidden fantasies be a regular occurrence?

Shaking her head at her crazy ideas, at thinking she could turn a wild fling into something more, she followed Aqua, Sloan and Sister Mary Katherine down the hall. After a brief knock on the door, Aqua strode into the office.

The two men inside, faced with a nun, a librarian, a historian, a dispatcher and a peach pie, had the only legitimate reaction available. They dropped their jaws.

Sloan propped her hand on her shapely hip. "Easy, boys. The Calvary is here."

"And we brought pie," Andrea added lamely.

To her surprise, Tyler moved toward her and folded her into his arms. "I'm so glad you're here."

He really was amazing.

It seemed impossible they'd been together less than a week. The distant fantasy she'd had in high school felt like another life, another guy. She knew Tyler inside now, and she liked him more as each layer was revealed. He wasn't perfect, yet he was.

But she worried she'd never be enough for him. Until recently, she never would have had the courage to live out her sensual fantasies. She lived in the past much of the time. She plodded along, watching, cataloging, assessing the treasures of others.

With a thief on the loose and an election hanging in the balance, though, her self-evaluation would have to wait. "You guys might want to know that the press corps is gathered outside."

Sloan examined her nails. "Jerry Mescle and Clyde do not make a corps."

"I'll have a talk with them later," the sheriff said, then smiled fiercely.

Andrea doubted the sheriff would have to say a word. That intense, blue-eyed stare would be enough to scare off the National Guard.

"Besides," Tyler began, "we have bigger issues to deal with. Namely, the city council's office, the mayor's office, community safety groups, neighborhood watch leaders and randomly annoyed islanders, all of whom have expressed concern about our ability to maintain law and order."

Andrea wanted to say something to comfort him, mostly private things. She settled with the reason for their visit. "Then it's probably good we've formed a task force."

Tyler grinned.

The sheriff groaned.

"Unofficially," Andrea added, casting a look at Sloan. Sloan simply stared at her father.

After a moment or two of this silent battle, he sighed. "We might as well go into the break room. There's a conference table in there."

Sister Mary Katherine, still holding the pie, smiled benignly and led the way.

Gathered with coffee and pie, Tyler brought everybody up to date on the case developments, including Dwayne finally locating Mrs. Jackson's pool boy, who he was interviewing now. Nobody seemed to think the easygoing surfer would have anything to add, though.

The boot print found at the church seemed likely to belong to the custodian, who admitted he owned a pair of work boots and had been fixing a crack in the sidewalk near the garden, likely the source of the mud.

There were no leads at the pawnshops, no witnesses coming forward. Tyler and the sheriff were both puzzled about the lack of evidence in all three cases. Even on such a small, close-knit island, nobody saw anything, heard anything or seemed to know anything about the thefts. The state crime lab was still working on fingerprint and fiber evidence from the church, so they were hopeful they'd have some leads next week.

"Of course by that time he might have already stolen the mayor's silverware right out of his hand during dinner," Tyler said.

"He's fast," Sloan said, drumming her fingernails on the table. "I'll give him that."

"What does the mayor say when he calls?" Andrea asked.

"It's not content," Tyler returned. "It's quantity. He calls about once an hour for updates."

The sheriff polished off his pie and leaned back in his chair. "The mayor needs to go back to the golf course where he belongs and let us do our jobs."

Tyler nodded. "He did. He called last hour from the fifth tee."

Sloan looked annoyed. "He could at least answer some of the panicked calls and reassure people."

"Everyone serves to their strengths," Sister Mary Katherine said with quiet authority.

"No disrespect, Sister," the sheriff put in, "but you haven't seen the mayor's lousy putting."

Andrea rose to refill everyone's coffee cups. "So, it's up to us."

"Any new developments on your end?" Tyler asked her.

"I put out the alert for the chalice, and my friends, even with their—" she sent a cautious look at the sister "—*flexible* moral codes, were very disturbed by a stolen church relic."

The sheriff studied her. "You're the fraud specialist?"

Andrea returned to her seat. "Yes, sir." Clearly, she'd surprised the sheriff. He only knew her as Sloan's quiet, nerdy friend, after all. "If any of the stolen items are sold, I'll hear about it."

"What if they're not sold?" Sloan asked.

Tyler shrugged. "Why steal if you're not going to profit?"

"There are people who just like to take things," Sister Mary Katherine pointed out. "Lost souls."

Aqua, who'd silently been taking notes on her laptop the entire time, stopped typing. "You might take something for revenge. When I caught my ex with another chick at a nightclub in Charleston, I stole the tires off his car."

The room went silent.

"I'm not sure I remember that on your résumé," the sheriff said, rubbing his chin.

Nonchalantly, Aqua resumed typing. "I gave them back. I just put them on his porch instead of on his car."

The sister clicked her tongue in admonishment. "Aqua, don't you think you could have come up with a more peaceful solution?"

"That *was* peaceful, Sister. I wanted to shoot the tires. And him."

"Aqua has a point," Andrea said, trying to shift the focus back to the case. If the good sister launched into one of her "do unto others" lessons, the meeting was going to run a little long. "Maybe the thief has somehow been wronged by the victims?"

"That brings us back to the sheriff's idea that we need to find a connection between the victims," Tyler said.

The sheriff lifted his mug. "It makes sense in a serial case."

"They all attend the church," the sister said.

"Like most of the island," Tyler reminded her.

Unfortunately, nobody could think of another commonality between the stolen pieces or their owners, except that the items were all silver—if only in color in the case of the trophy—and all gone without a trace.

The tea set and chalice were priceless and had historical significance to the island. The trophy worthless except as a symbol of victory.

Symbols? Did all three of the items represent some as yet unknown desire? History? Faith? Cups to drink out of?

And the victims. What about them?

They were a rich elderly lady, a maniac volleyball captain and the church. How did they—

Andrea halted her thoughts. Hang on. *Two* rich, elderly ladies' homes had been broken into. The trophy belonged to Cal Wells, but the house was owned by his mother.

So how did the church fit? Other than being the ladies' choice of worship, it didn't. The property and buildings were owned by the Catholic Church, not one individual.

Still, the Church itself was well-off. It seemed disrespectful to say "rich," since their budget was reserved for worship and community service, but there were those who might resent the power and money. Hadn't arguments over faith toppled governments, aristocracies and led to long, bloody wars throughout history?

"Maybe it's about money," she found herself saying.

"So why take Cal's worthless volleyball trophy?" Sloan asked reasonably.

"Maybe it isn't the items but the victims," Andrea said. "They all have money. Maybe the thief resents power and wealth."

Tyler cleared his throat. "There's certainly a link between the women and the church."

"It seems to be the only link," the sheriff said, clearly frustrated.

Andrea swallowed, knowing only too well about a link between Mrs. Jackson and Mrs. Wells. "They both get meals delivered a couple times a week from the church."

Sitting beside Andrea, Sloan linked their hands. "Nobody thinks Finn is responsible for this."

Both Tyler and Sister Mary Katherine smiled confidently.

"But we have to add Finn to the mix," Aqua said, ever blunt. "The thief wanted him to get blamed. So the thief has to know him."

"Or at least know *of* him," Tyler added.

"And if this guy resents money, he's on the wrong island," Sloan said, frowning. "We barely have property that isn't beachfront."

"It could be an outsider," Aqua said.

"Who knew about the sacraments closet at the church?" Tyler shook his head. "Not likely."

"So it's an islander who's taking the symbols of wealth?" Andrea ventured. "What about Lester Cradock?" She'd long been concerned about the timing and the election. "He's an activist. You said so yourself, Tyler."

"He certainly wouldn't mind disrupting the election," Sloan said in agreement.

"But the trophy still doesn't fit," Aqua argued.

Tyler and the sheriff exchanged a look. "We could run him, just in case. Especially since *nothing* seems to fit all the facts."

"But something does," the sheriff said, rising.

His height and imposing presence always commanded a room. Today, Andrea felt his comfort. And his determination.

This was the man Tyler would be. Not the same, since Tyler was more easygoing. His strength was more understated, his fierceness usually covered with charm. But the respect and confidence was the same. The islanders would value him, and he would always present himself with self-assurance.

Between Tyler, the sheriff and the task force, this thief didn't stand a chance.

"Let's draw up a plan for dealing with the immediate issues," the sheriff continued. "The evidence is still comin' in. We're bound to get a break."

There was a rushed but decisive discussion on holding a town hall meeting to answer questions and calm the residents' fears.

The sheriff nodded. "Excellent idea. Tyler, you'll take the lead."

"I—" A rapid battle of pleasure and panic crossed Tyler's face, one Andrea was sure only she understood the full depths of. "I'd be honored," he said finally.

As the summit ended, everyone was given an area of responsibility to deal with and report back on.

Sister Mary Katherine was in charge of organizing the neighborhood watch groups. Sloan and her historical society members were going house to house to warn owners of other island treasures that might be at risk and offer to store the items in the bank's vault. Aqua offered to go through the call log over the last few months to see if anyone had called with a complaint about seeing anything or anyone out of place in the weeks leading up to each theft.

Andrea was asked to research the stolen items, where and when they were made, who'd owned them, their insurance policies and estimate a current dollar value.

In absentia, Dwayne was put in charge of documentation, and Tyler and Sheriff Caldwell vowed to handle strategy and were cocaptains of the investigation. So as everyone trickled out, and the sheriff left to "talk" to the press—after which he was going to Mabel's to thank her for the pie—Andrea found herself alone with Tyler.

He sat on the conference table and drew her between his legs. His thoughts had to be on the case, but his eyes burned with an intensity that jumped into a more personal area.

"It's a good plan," she said, still unsure of his mood.

"Mmm." He tugged her closer, kissing the side of her neck. "We'll find the guy."

"So you're not worried about closing the case?"

His lips trailed toward her ear. "No."

"Or the election?"

He flicked his tongue against her earlobe. "No way."

Desire shot through her body.

Maybe she didn't have to plod today. Enjoying him before she left for London, and he simply lost interest in her, was important.

So, outside the commitment of a belly-button ring like Aqua's, but somewhere near the concept of sex in a squad car, she could be a bit wild. For now.

She laid her hands on his shoulders, reconsidered, but then sent one of them southward.

Hardening instantly, he sucked in a breath.

"I've been thinking about fantasies," she said softly, stroking him.

"Yeah?" His voice was little more than a squeak.

"Remember how we broke several traffic laws in the squad car last night?"

His erection pulsed. "Vividly."

"Well, there's another one where I get naked in the sheriff's office."

"We're not in the sheriff's office."

She grabbed the hem of her sundress and lifted it over her head. "Then we'll have to make do with what we've got."

13

THE NEXT WEEK PASSED in a blur.

The state crime lab had processed the evidence from the cases, but unfortunately no one had the urge to say *By jove, I think we've got it!*

Come to think of it, Andrea couldn't think of many places where that *would* be an appropriate phrase to use. Maybe the Theatre Royal in London.

The task force met every night to discuss case developments, strategies and rumors. Kirk, the pool guy, was eliminated officially, since he had a rock-solid alibi for the days surrounding the theft at the church—he'd been in Myrtle Beach for a surfing competition. After winning, he'd used his celebration time to accept free drinks from various fans, who were only too happy to supply details of the bar and hotel room crawl.

Personally, Andrea could have lived without the details, especially since she didn't find anything to surpass her recent tendency to act out her sexual fantasies with Tyler.

Aqua and Dwayne followed up on the financial status and whereabouts of Simon Iverson, Mrs. Jackson's nephew, plus Cal Wells and Roger Bampton. Iverson was vaguely "at home alone" on each of the nights. Did he not have a social life, or was there more to see with him? He was doing okay financially, but they'd uncovered an extravagant purchase of a sixty-eight-foot yacht, which had seriously cut into his savings.

Interestingly, neither Wells nor Bampton had substantiated alibis for any of the nights. Could Wells have stolen his own trophy to divert suspicion away from himself? Had Roger Bampton taken the loss of the volleyball championship so hard he'd stolen the trophy? And why would either man take the tea set or the chalice? They were both very well-off financially.

Lester Cradock did have a solid alibi for at least two of the thefts—he'd been leading gun-control rallies at the state capitol in Columbia.

After the town hall meeting, the newspaper had again printed a story designed to ignite the island to riot status. While no one took things that seriously, Jerry Mescle's exaggerated writing had driven people to pick up the phone and call the sheriff's office, delaying progress in the already-bogged-down investigation.

Still, there were quite a few supporters who'd attended Tyler's campaign rally last night. At Andrea's suggestion, and given the vitriolic atmosphere, she'd suggested food-based giveaways. So the free pie, courtesy of Gilda, plus the free fried chicken, courtesy of Mabel, and the coffee bar/real bar had both been hits—particularly since they'd served the statewide vodka-infused phenomenon known as Firefly Sweet Tea.

It tasted like Granny's traditionally iced and sugared concoction until the consumers found their heads spinning in a way their elders probably never intended. But it made for a great party.

The stories of the thefts were the talk of the island with

a single exception. Everyone was twittering to report a previously impossible turn of events—Misty and Dwayne were dating.

They'd shown up Friday night at Coconut Joe's without Jack, sharing virgin piña coladas and a shrimp dip appetizer, then enjoying Joe's famous fried flounder. Saturday night they'd returned with Jack, and following dinner the trio had walked into the sunset on the beach below.

Andrea doubted Jerry was planning a story about romantic happy endings.

"Andrea?"

Turning from the balcony, she walked into her bedroom. A familiar sight greeted her—bare-chested and dark hair rumpled, Tyler was propped on one elbow and looking at her with a sleepy, confused expression.

"Did the phone ring?" he asked.

"No." Amazed as always to find him more and more attractive, she sat on the bed beside him. "I just woke up early. I was thinking about the case."

After linking their fingers, he flopped back onto the pillows. "Isn't it Saturday?"

"Yes."

"And I'm not on duty?"

"No."

Tugging her on top of him, he wrapped his arms around her and rolled her beneath him in the space of a heartbeat. "Then there are much more interesting things to do than think."

He parted her robe and skimmed his lips across the bare skin he exposed. As his lips closed over her nipple, she arched her back and pressed her hands against his shoulders.

Her pulse blasted off as desire surged through her.

He could do that with a look or a word. His touch was almost too much.

She had no idea how she'd find level ground again. Everything was centered on him, the pleasure he brought, the hope and hunger that blossomed in her chest.

With lots of practice, he rolled on a condom, never stopping in the laving kisses at her breast. He was an amazing multitasker, she decided, her breathing reduced to pants.

Her climax rushed on, somehow still unexpected with its intensity. As he followed her, his face buried in her hair, she held on and couldn't help but wonder how important he'd become, how much of her daily life was wrapped around and inside him.

How had she let that happen?

Over the last week he'd practically moved in. They'd live in a bubble of pleasure, even as chaos swirled around them. Her brother's future was still in question; she was due to leave the country on an extended assignment in four days; a thief was on the loose and the all-important election would be decided on Tuesday.

"Are you still with me?" Tyler asked, his voice raw and tender.

Lying alongside him, she pressed her lips to his chest. "I'm here."

But how had she gotten here? What was she doing with him? Where were they going?

"Are you nervous about the election?" she asked, pushing her own troubled thoughts aside.

"A little."

"Don't worry. You'll win. And if something really strange happens, any town would be lucky to have you."

He shook his head. "I'm not going anywhere. I'm home for good."

"Not tempted to fly off and see more of the world?"

"Nope." Smoothing her hair off her face, he kissed the tip of her nose. "I can't go anywhere. I'd have to leave you."

Her pulse spiked. "You can't choose where you live based on me."

"Sure I can. You're the most important person in my life."

Andrea was struck completely silent. Her heart pounded with excitement. Or maybe it was disbelief.

She focused on the sincere expression in his bright blue eyes. No, it was fear slamming through her. Definitely fear.

"But you're—" She stopped, shook her head and tried again. "We're—"

"Amazing together?" He cupped her face, kissing her softly. "Extremely compatible in bed? We trust and support each other. We like the same foods and TV shows."

"We're completely wrong for each other," she finished in a blurted rush.

"Well, then that's a real problem, seeing as I'm in love with you."

She didn't climb off the bed, she leaped. He loved her? Really? He definitely *loved* her.

No way.

Confused and naked, she grabbed the first thing her hand fumbled for, which turned out to be his T-shirt. "You can't be," she said, her pulse in a full panic as she pulled on the shirt, wincing as the scent of his cologne wafted to her nose.

"'Fraid I am," he said, sitting up to rest on the pillows behind his back as if settling in for a long discussion.

"But you're a fantasy," she practically shouted in accusation. "You're not real. *This* isn't real."

Anger jumped into his eyes. "Sorry to disappoint you, baby, but I'm real, and so are my feelings."

"But you're supposed to be with some blonde, big-boobed cheerleader."

Even as she said the words, they sounded stupid. And yet, that was the vision she'd always had for his future. The realistic one, not the fantasy where the two of them rode off into the beach-shadowed sunset on his motorcycle, a stallion or in a Corvette, depending on which scenario she favored in the moment.

"You're blonde," he said tightly. "I like your boobs just fine, and if you want to cheer, I'll be happy to buy you some pom-poms and a short skirt."

She turned away. "They wouldn't fit me."

Behind her, he was silent for a long while. "And I don't either, huh?"

Looking back over her shoulder, she met his gaze and tried to make him—and her susceptible heart—understand. "I'm leaving in a few days. This was supposed to be uncomplicated fun."

He stared at her hard. "I was supposed to satisfy you, then go on my merry way."

Exactly. But she couldn't say so. Was that because she didn't want to hurt him, or because she didn't even believe her own delusions anymore?

"I'm not really like this," she felt obligated to explain. "I don't indulge in fantasies or take risks. I work in insurance."

"No kidding? Sex in the squad car, in the conference room?"

"Those were…isolated incidents. I've never done anything like that with a man before."

"I'm glad I was such an inspiration, but those *isolated incidents* didn't seem like big risks to me. Maybe because I love you and hoped you'd eventually feel the same way."

She closed her eyes briefly. She couldn't care so much about him. What if he got tired of her? *If?* Hell, when.

Rising, he slid on a pair of jeans laying beside the bed. His motions were stiff, and, when he looked at her, his eyes remote. "You live in the past, Andrea. You work there, you *dwell* there. I've apologized for the boy I was—and remember I was a boy—in every way I can think of. I trusted you with secrets, fears and worries I've never shared with anyone. If you can't believe in me now, then I guess all we've had was some great fantasy sex."

He started toward the door. "But then that's all you were after all along, right?"

She didn't know what she really wanted. Nothing had gone the way she'd planned, and she still wasn't sure if that was a good thing or not. "Tyler, I—"

"Andy!"

Finn.

"Be right there!" Andrea shouted back as she yanked off Tyler's shirt. Tossing it at him, she darted into her closet for something of her own to wear.

By the time she returned to the bedroom, she wore a blousy, lace top and red Capri jeans. Tyler had taken the abrupt hint and put on his shirt, though he didn't meet her gaze as they walked downstairs.

Was she crazy or smart?

How could they expect to build a real relationship on the stranger fantasy she'd initiated? In her teenage mind, he'd meant everything. Her entire world had been him. She couldn't go back there.

"What's up?" Tyler asked her brother with forced casualness when they reached the bottom of the stairs.

"I have some news about the silver case." Finn's gaze flicked to Andrea's. "I didn't mean to interrupt."

Tyler looked at her over his shoulder. "It was nothing."

The love he'd proclaimed earlier wasn't anywhere evident in his eyes. She wasn't surprised, but her heart broke, just a little more wide open than it had before, and she wondered if she hadn't completely ruined everything this time.

Tyler made coffee while Andrea and Finn settled in at the kitchen table.

Resolutely, he blocked the conversation Finn had walked into.

There was no way the woman he loved had told him he meant nothing to her. She hadn't rejected him; she hadn't looked at him with shock and dread.

He'd trusted her with everything, and she hadn't just backed up, she'd run away.

Alongside the cookie sheets, he found a tray that he used to carry the mugs of coffee to the table. A chill infused the fall air, but he didn't need any more clothes. His anger and disappointment kept him warm.

Careful not to look at Andrea, even though she was mere inches away, he lifted his steaming mug and stared at Finn. "What did you find out?"

Finn's gaze darted between Tyler and his sister. "Are you sure everything's okay?"

"Fine," Tyler said.

"Fine," Andrea echoed at the same time.

"O-kay…" Finn picked up his coffee mug and drank.

With a grimace, he set down the cup again. "Dude, you got a thing against sugar?"

Anticipating this reaction, Tyler pushed forward the sugar bowl and spoon he'd brought on the tray. "Go crazy."

After dumping in at least five teaspoons, Finn pronounced his coffee perfect. "So, here's the thing…" He shifted his gaze between Tyler and Andrea. "It may not even be important."

"But you think it is," Tyler said. Even only knowing Finn a couple of weeks, he'd learned the guy didn't say much that wasn't significant.

Finn nodded. "Yeah. A guy I work with told me he'd talked to that volleyball captain Roger Bampton about the church's meal delivery schedule. He asked specifically about the Wells house."

"How did this conversation come up?" Tyler asked casually, though the tips of his fingers tingled.

"I said to my friend how crazy this whole missing chalice thing is. You know, cops at the church." He lifted his shoulders, then let them fall.

"Go on."

"My friend said something like, yeah, something crazy happened to him, too. He had dudes comin' up to him, offering to do his job." As Finn paused, his gaze met Tyler's. "Long as he took the fifty and didn't say anything."

The tingle turned into a full-fledged buzz.

"You're saying Roger Bampton offered your friend fifty bucks to deliver a meal to Mrs. Wells in the weeks before the theft of the trophy?"

"Yep."

"And asked him to keep this transaction secret?"

"Yep."

Tyler set his coffee cup on the table. His mind raced

through the possibilities as he tried to line up the facts and evidence with this new revelation.

"I can see Roger getting mad about the volleyball tournament and taking the trophy," Andrea said, speaking for the first time since they'd sat down. "Well, sort of. I mean, taking the trophy still doesn't make him a winner. But why would he take the tea set and chalice?"

"To throw off suspicion of the real crime," Finn said as if that were obvious.

Tyler considered the idea, which they'd actually floated around the task force meetings—though the trophy had been seen as the diversionary tactic, not the real crime. "As a distraction it seems pretty over-the-top to take priceless treasures to cover up stealing a worthless trophy."

"Or really smart," Finn said, leaning forward. "You guys are knocking yourselves out looking for somebody who needs money or a theft ring after historical artifacts." He managed a rueful smile. "Or an ex-con who can't give up the old game. You're not looking at dumpy ole Roger."

Aqua had compared the volleyball tournament to the Yankees–Red Sox rivalry. Could this trophy really mean so much? Wasn't that seriously delusional?

Then he remembered the shouting match at the station, the passion and fury on Roger's reddened face as he'd accused Cal Wells of cheating. Could Finn's scenario be the answer?

"I got a comparison," Finn continued. "Once, the gang wanted to boost a rival gang member's car. We didn't want the car, we just wanted to get our hands on it and mess it up."

"Finn!" Andrea shouted.

"Let him finish," Tyler said to her, being careful not to look in her direction. With their relationship crashing, all he had to focus on was his job, so he might as well do it effectively.

"All in the past," Finn said, holding up his hands in surrender. "Anyway, to boost the car, we had to create a distraction, so we took tire irons and busted the window of a fancy jewelry store. Alarms went screaming. Cops and employees running around in a panic. During the melee, on the next block over, we roll away in the car without a peep."

"I really didn't need to know all this," Andrea said dryly.

Oddly enough, Tyler did. The cops could learn a thing or two from the bad guys. Well, former bad guys. Didn't Andrea use ex-thieves as informants in her business?

"That's pretty smart," Tyler said, looking at Finn in a whole new light.

Finn ducked his head. "Yeah, but not in a good way, I guess."

"Definitely in a good way," Tyler said, rising. "I should get back to the station and work on this new development."

Finn stood as well. "So I helped?"

Tyler clapped his hand on the younger man's shoulder. "You did."

"Helped?" Andrea said, standing beside them, a proud smile on her face. "You solved the case, Finn."

"I don't know about that," Finn said.

"You've given us the break we've been looking for," Tyler assured him. "In fact, you could help some more. It's easy enough to guess how Roger stole the trophy, but we'll need a lot more evidence to prove he stole the tea set and chalice. Why don't we head to Mrs. Jackson's house and talk to her?"

"Great idea." Andrea headed toward the door.

Tyler stiffened. He needed to concentrate on the case. On anything besides her rejection. "I think Finn and I can handle this," he said as he walked by her into the hallway.

Damn, he'd even fallen in love with the house in the last few weeks. The old wood and the new paint. The sound of crashing waves, the star-strewn view from her bedroom balcony.

"But I'm on the task force," Andrea argued.

"It's okay, isn't it, Andy?" Finn asked, saving Tyler from coming up with a lame excuse to escape without her. "I'd kind of like to see this through. This cop stuff is kind of cool."

Andrea's gaze moved to Tyler, but he looked away. "Yeah, sure. I think you'll be more help than me, anyway."

14

As Tyler steered the patrol car toward the Jackson house, he figured if the truth was going to come out, it might as well all come out. "I'm in love with your sister."

Finn barked out a laugh. "No kidding."

"How long have you known?"

"Since you said you thought I was innocent, even though you had no reason to back that up. How long have you known?"

So much for unexpected revelations. "Right about that same time."

"You gonna marry her?"

His heart jumped to his throat, then settled. "I guess. Someday. Maybe."

"You guess, someday, maybe?" Finn shook his head. "I heard you were good with the ladies. Boy, did I ever get that wrong."

"We haven't known each other very long. Don't you think a proposal would be rushing things?"

"She told me you've known each other since high school."

"Good point."

"How long do you need? Seriously, dude, what are you waiting for?"

Tyler said nothing for several minutes. "You're very decisive."

"When you've been in prison, you learn to focus on the stuff that really matters."

Tyler glanced at Finn, who'd turned his head to stare out the window. The simplicity of the sky overhead and the sun beating down was something Tyler took for granted.

What *was* he waiting for?

Oh, yeah, some idea that the woman he loved might actually want to be with him past next week. Some sign that she cared about him. Some signal that he meant more than a series of fantasy nights.

He'd never told a woman he loved her before. Didn't she know how hard it was for him to realize that one person, above all others, could make or break his life? To know that he'd never truly be happy without her by his side?

How could she know that, you dummy? You were too busy getting angry.

We're compatible in bed? We like the same TV shows?

Who the hell cared about stupid stuff like that? Could he have been any less romantic?

It took the honesty of youth. *You guess, someday, maybe.*

That would most certainly not be his answer to getting Andrea to understand and believe in his love.

"Thanks for bringing me along," Finn said, breaking into his thoughts.

"I could use the help." *In more ways than just the case.*

"Especially since you needed to escape from Andy."

No point in pretending otherwise. "Right."

"You guys have a fight?"

"Sort of. Can we focus on the case right now?"

"Sure. One last thing, though. I know a great jeweler."

Tyler cast him a sideways glance. "You do, huh?"

"Jeez. A legit one."

"Thanks." Though he thought jewelry was premature when she wouldn't believe he loved her. "I'll keep that in mind. Did you just happen to find out this information about Roger from your friend, or were you questioning him? Unofficially, of course."

"Unofficially, I was questioning him."

"Nice job. Why?"

Finn's face was set in stubborn lines Tyler recognized easily. "Nobody's going to take me seriously until this case is closed."

"No, they're not." Wouldn't he do the same if his innocence was in question? Tyler tossed over his cell phone/PDA. "Call the station and ask Aqua to e-mail me a picture of Roger Bampton for us to show Mrs. Jackson."

"No need. I've got a picture on my phone. I used it with my buddy to identify Roger earlier."

Impressed that Finn had taken such an initiative, Tyler wondered if his name shouldn't be on Tuesday's ballot. Maybe someday it would be.

When they arrived at Mrs. Jackson's house, the elderly lady offered them lemonade, which they politely declined, and Tyler made sure he kept himself between their theft victim and the budding young detective. The last thing he needed was to explain to Andrea how her brother had been propositioned during his first official interrogation.

Well, at least the first one where he hadn't been interrogated himself.

"Do you recognize this man?" Tyler asked Mrs. Jackson, holding up Finn's cell phone.

"Oh, well…" She leaned sideways, her gaze flitting to

Finn, who stood just behind Tyler's left shoulder. "I certainly recognize *that* one. So polite. And strong. Carrying those heavy lunch containers all by himself."

"Mrs. Jackson," Tyler said, blocking her view. "The man in the picture?"

"Oh, well…I'm not really sure," she said, squinting at the screen.

She was ninety-three, after all.

"Do you have a computer, Mrs. Jackson?" Finn asked her, stepping forward.

After sending Finn a flirtatious smile, she extended her hand toward the back of the house. "My nephew set it up in the kitchen. I'm supposed to send pictures of water fowl to my grandnieces and nephews in Chicago, but I find the Internet full of other…stimulating information."

No one, not even Andrea in her skimpiest lingerie, could get Tyler to ask about that stimulation.

In the kitchen, Finn set himself up at the wide, flat-screen monitor and found several pictures of Roger Bampton on the island's volleyball league Web site. Tyler recognized the one Finn had downloaded to his phone.

Smart, decisive, technologically savvy and could think like a criminal? The guy was destined for law enforcement.

"Have you ever seen this man, Mrs. Jackson?" Finn asked with a facial blowup of Roger Bampton on the screen.

"Oh, sure, I know him. He's the president of the cleaning service I use."

Tyler exchanged a glance with Finn. "He's been in your house?" he asked, keeping his voice steady, giving away none of the excitement of discovery he felt.

Mrs. Jackson nodded. "Sure. He came by to get a new key. The old one had been destroyed in a fire."

"Fire?" Tyler prompted.

"The offices at the cleaning company." She shook her head. "A shame. There was a lightning storm. So I gave him a new key, and the girls came by the next day like always."

Tyler just bet they had.

Finn pointed at the screen. "Mrs. Jackson, this is Rog—"

"Thank you," Tyler interrupted. "We'll get back to you when we have further information about your tea set."

Mrs. Jackson pursed her lips. "The sheriff's back now, so I have no doubt my property will be returned, safe and sound."

"You called him away from his vacation, didn't you, ma'am?" Tyler asked, though he already knew the answer.

Her eyes turned sly. "Why would you want to go to Bermuda when you have this beautiful island right here?"

"I can't imagine," Tyler returned, though not without some irony. The sheriff would welcome his retirement in many ways, not the least of which was scowling at Tyler right at this moment. "I hope I can count on your vote Tuesday," he said as they headed toward the door.

Mrs. Jackson raised her wrinkled chin. "Lester Cradock promised he'd get rid of the alien invaders with his bull-whip."

So Tyler wasn't getting everybody's support. He had much bigger concerns, so he shrugged off the criticism and walked with Finn back to the patrol car.

"Why'd you stop me from telling Mrs. Jackson about Roger's guilt?" Finn asked as they backed out of the driveway.

"Cops don't determine guilt."

"But Roger bribed my buddy, he got a key to Mrs. Jackson's house. He took everything. He's the thief."

"Sure he is. But Mrs. Jackson will be called as a witness

at some point." Though Tyler anticipated he could avoid a full trial with the information they'd gathered. Frankly, he didn't see Roger Bampton standing up to a full-on police interrogation. "We have her statement, which can be added to the evidence, but we don't tell her what we're thinking or where we're going. Let the prosecutor build the case."

"But she pretty much guaranteed Roger's guilt."

Tyler shifted his gaze to Finn. "And if you were me, would you want her to know that? The woman who convinced big, bad Buddy Caldwell to cut his vacation short?"

Finn's eyes widened. "Oh, well, no. I guess not."

"Besides," Tyler added as he pulled into the lot at city hall, "the police gather and present evidence. The court and jury determine guilt. Remember that when you become a cop."

"Who said I wanted to be a cop?" Finn asked, a little too casually to be believed.

"Nobody." Tyler swung out of the patrol car and headed up the stone steps to the station. "By the way, if you decide to give up life as a church errand guy, I'd be proud to have you as a deputy."

Finn halted. His face broke into the first genuine smile Tyler had seen on him since he'd met the young man.

"Thanks," Finn replied. "You know you haven't won yet, though, right?"

Tyler's thoughts flicked briefly to Andrea, of the dreams he had with her. Of the way she'd stood by him through everything, then turned away from the best part of him— his heart. He didn't know how to convince her to believe in them when she was running from the promise of the future, settling for the past.

But he knew he couldn't let her go to London without trying. And, if she did leave, he wanted to remind her there was something wonderful to come home to. Something that could overcome the past. Something romantic and true. Something to let her know that he was a man who always got what he wanted, and if he was a hero, it was because of her.

"Don't worry," he said to Finn. "I'll win."

"You can come in," Andrea said to her best friend, "but I'm packing."

Turning from the door, Andrea headed across the foyer and up the stairs, knowing Sloan would follow.

"You're actually running away?"

"I'm going on a trip. To London. For work. In two days."

"How decisive of you."

"This assignment's been planned for months."

"And you're telling me if Finn's guilt on this silver case was in question, if there was even the slightest chance he might be arrested, you'd still be going?"

At the top of the steps, Andrea turned and faced her friend, wishing she could face herself so easily. She wouldn't be going anywhere if the case wasn't closed, and Sloan knew that as well as she did.

The silver stealer case, however, was indeed closed.

Confronted with the evidence Tyler, Finn and the rest of the task force had gathered, Roger Bampton had confessed and handed over the stolen items—kept in a box beneath his bed—to the police. He'd been arraigned and officially charged the day before. Though a trial date had been set, a rumor was already floating around that a deal would be made in which Roger might avoid jail time.

Supposedly, Sister Mary Katherine was encouraging

probation, though she did suggest his scrubbing of the restrooms in city hall—with a toothbrush—might be an excellent penance and form of community service.

Andrea thought he also needed some serious counseling, since the master thief really had stolen two priceless island treasures in order to throw the police off about who'd want the volleyball trophy—namely, him. And, oddly enough, her theory about the significant timing of the thefts, coinciding with the election, turned out to be true in a way, since Roger had planned his crimes months in advance, but saved the actual execution until the sheriff left on vacation.

Sheepishly, he'd admitted he hadn't been prepared for Tyler's tenacity and quick action.

Personally, Andrea wanted to kick Roger's butt off the island to some dark, dank prison where some big, bald, tattooed and scary guy was liable to adopt him as his little woman, but maybe that was simply bitterness over him putting her, her brother and her lover through hell for the last two weeks.

Former lover, her conscience reminded her.

"I'm going to London," she said finally to Sloan, heading into her bedroom.

"Packing on election day. How…ridiculous. 'Cause, gee, I don't know if you've heard, but today was important for a close friend of yours. Oh, no. Wait. He's more than a friend. He's the love of your freakin' life."

Since the last was delivered in a determined, annoyed and exasperated tone, Andrea couldn't help but wince, though she didn't pause from pulling a sweater set from her closet.

Maybe she was miserable without him, maybe she wondered—though only every other ten seconds—whether she'd made a huge mistake in turning away from him.

Was she protecting her heart at the risk of losing a chance at complete happiness?

"I voted," Andrea said, tucking the sweater in her suitcase, which was laid open on her bed. She tapped the flag sticker on her chest. "What more am I supposed to do?"

Sloan crossed her arms. "How about holding his hand as the results come in?"

"You're honestly concerned Lester Cradock is going to make a last-minute surge and win the election?"

Sloan wasn't deterred. "Then you could be at my house, helping me decorate for the victory party. We have streamers, balloons and confetti, plus tons of food. There's a stage, a band and—"

"I'm not coming." Andrea started toward her closet.

Sloan stepped in front of her. "You need to be there. He needs your support."

"How do you know that?"

"He told me."

Her heart jumped, like a betrayer of her body. "You talked to him?"

"A little. He wouldn't say much." Sloan tapped her stiletto-clad foot. "Clearly, he was upset."

"What did he say?"

"That you'd argued and basically broken up. Is that what happened?"

"Basically."

Sloan snorted. "You dumped him."

"Yes," Andrea admitted, her stomach clenching.

"Have you lost your mind? You can't tell me you're not crazy about him."

Andrea yanked a jacket from a hanger. "Of course I'm crazy about him! I'm too crazy about him."

Sloan was silent.

Andrea tucked several more things in her suitcase. If she kept moving, if she had several thousand miles between her and Tyler, she was sure she'd come to her senses and remember that he was only going to break her heart again. Why should she hang around for that torture?

Sloan darted between Andrea and the suitcase. "That is absolutely the stupidest thing I've ever heard. You love him. You've loved him for years."

"I don't. I won't."

"And the best part," Sloan added as if she hadn't heard Andrea's protest, "is that he loves you, too."

But did he? They'd had a fantasy affair. How could any permanence come from that?

Exhausted from worry and lack of sleep. Andrea flopped on the bed. Was she being smart or stubborn? "So he said."

Sloan held up her hand. "Hold on. He told you he loved you? When did this happen?"

"Saturday."

"Okay," Sloan said, striding from one end of the room to the other, then back again. Finally, she sat next to Andrea, holding her hand gently between her own. "Okay," she repeated, her voice quiet, soothing. "Here's how it's going to be…. You're going to fix your hair, put on lip gloss and perfume, then you're going to get dressed in something festive, sparkly and hot. You're coming with me to my house. There, you'll greet Tyler at the door with a celebratory glass of champagne, an apology for being such an idiot and a kiss designed to ignite the new silver star on his chest."

"Why would I do that?"

"'Cause if you don't, I'm going to kick your stupid butt from here to London." Sloan smiled fiercely. "No plane ticket or baggage check-in required."

Jumping to her feet, Andrea flung her hands in the air. "It's not real. We've been having sex for two weeks. We've been living a fantasy. My life is supposed to change. What, I'm suddenly worthy of the hero of the island based on a costume and a few hot nights?"

"Yes."

Sloan's resolute answer made Andrea's heart contract. She'd wanted him for so long, but on some level, she'd never believed he could be hers. In her teenage fantasies, he'd been the ideal, the pinnacle, something the math nerd could never hope to claim.

But she was an adult now. Did she really want to live in the past forever?

"He should be with somebody else," she said, though her argument seemed weak even in her own mind.

"Who? Somebody smarter? Prettier? More loyal? Someone who loves him more?"

No one could love him more.

The truth pounded through her as solid and real as the waves pounded the shore outside her window.

With that singular truth glaring at her, she also realized she hadn't loved him back in high school. She'd been obsessed with him. But her obsession hadn't been real. *It* had been the fantasy. The man she'd spent the last few weeks with was the real Tyler, the one who had hopes and fears, strengths and weaknesses.

He hadn't done anything but be himself, and she'd held herself back all by herself. He'd trusted her with his innermost thoughts and secrets. He'd trusted her brother when he had no reason to except on her word. He'd been demonstrating how important she was every moment since he'd handed her champagne at the costume ball.

But instead of believing in him when it mattered the most, she'd rejected him. Unconscious revenge for him rejecting her years ago? If so, she couldn't have been more wrong.

A tough admission for the woman who thought she knew so much.

"He really loves me, doesn't he?" she said, rising.

Smiling, Sloan squeezed her hand. "He does."

"Then I guess I've got a party to go to."

15

TYLER STOOD NEAR THE STAGE, which had been set up beside the patriotically decorated gazebo in the backyard of Batherton Mansion.

Though he was grateful to Aiden and Sloan for providing the venue, and the citizens of Palmer's Island for electing him and helping him secure his family legacy, he didn't see the one face he longed to among the celebratory crowd.

She wasn't coming.

Sloan had left earlier to find Andrea and make sure she came to the victory party, but obviously she hadn't been successful.

He'd wanted to share this with her, the first introduction of him as sheriff to his hometown. She was the only one who'd truly understand how much the victory meant to him and how seriously he took the welfare and future of his fellow islanders to heart.

Hundreds of people milled around the yard and through the house, arguing about other elections around the state, agreeing about the wildlife preservation decree that had been passed.

He watched them huddle in groups, enjoying the food and drinks his generous friends had provided. They passed by in patriotic clothes, or—at least in the case of Jerry

Mescle—stood to the side and watched the proceedings with a gimlet eye. The press, it seemed, would always be there, fair or foul, peace or controversy.

Even Lester was having a good time. He'd somehow connected with the historical film society and was showing off his trademark bullwhip.

Tyler was proud, hopeful and…miserable. How was he supposed to make his dreams come true like this?

As his parents approached, he straightened his shoulders. "We're so proud of you," his mother said, kissing his cheek.

"Thanks, Mama." He hugged her, then leaned into his father as he wrapped his arm around his shoulders. "Where's Grandad?"

His father grinned. "He got waylaid by Lester. Something about physics and bullwhips. We slipped away."

Tyler found the energy to smile. "Smart move."

"You'll make a great sheriff, son," his father said. "Maybe even better than Dad."

As Andrea suggested, Tyler had told his parents and grandfather about the failed mission and the true reason for his retirement. They'd been sympathetic and understanding, as he should have expected them to be all along.

Tyler met his father's gaze. "Thanks. Though I guess you know your support hasn't stopped Grandad or Sheriff Caldwell from giving me advice every fifteen seconds."

His mother patted his cheek. "They'll let you do things your own way." Her eyes, identical to his, turned fierce. "Or they'll hear from me."

His family would stand by him, no matter what. He only wished Andrea could do the same. *Where was she?*

As his parents drifted back to the party and more islanders approached to congratulate him, he could listen with only half his attention. The rest was focusing on Plan B. If Andrea wasn't coming to him, he'd have to find a way to escape his own victory celebration and find her. He had no idea how he was going to convince her his love was real and forever, but there had to be a way.

Was the ring box in his jacket pocket too bold and too fast, or just right?

"Don't worry, Sheriff," Aidan said as he approached, pressing a glass of whiskey in his hands. "Sloan will come through."

"I'm not so sure," Tyler returned. He gratefully sipped the smoky whiskey. "Not that I don't have faith in Sloan. I just can't seem to reach Andrea."

"You guys have moved pretty fast."

"And that's bad?"

"No, it's just that Andrea's not much for impulsiveness."

With the times they'd acted out her fantasies fresh in his mind, Tyler could argue that point but decided not to. He knew what Aidan was trying to say—she wasn't naturally impulsive. So she was pretending with him?

That didn't bode well for his plans.

"She's got some crazy idea that my feelings for her won't last," Tyler admitted. "She doesn't take me seriously."

Aidan's knowing gaze cut to his. "Where did she get that idea?"

"Probably because I've never been serious about a woman before. But things have changed. *I've* changed."

"That happens when the right woman storms into your life."

Tyler glanced at his friend. "Did Sloan storm?"

"Oh, yeah."

"But then she fell into your arms and that was that."

Aidan, who nobody could accuse of being the jovial type, laughed. "Not exactly." He clapped Tyler on the shoulder. "Don't give up. You'll—"

"Excellent whiskey, Aidan," Carr Hamilton said, joining them and raising his glass. "I may have to switch brands."

Tyler stiffened. Though Andrea had assured him there was nothing personal between her and the suave attorney, he couldn't seem to get past his resentment of the guy.

"Congratulations, Sheriff," Hamilton said, toasting him.

Tyler nodded. "Thanks."

"I hear our girl is going to London. I guess you'll now be free to check out all the other female delights the island has to offer."

Tyler clenched his jaw. "By *our* girl, you certainly can't mean Andrea. She belongs to me."

To his surprise, Hamilton smiled. "Finn's right. You do love her."

"You bet I do, and if you come within ten feet of—"

"Hold on." Hamilton lifted his hands in peace. "Andrea is my friend. I don't know you very well. I'm just looking out for her best interests."

"Then that's me," Tyler said firmly.

Hamilton glanced around. "And yet she doesn't seem to be here by your side."

Tyler's shoulders slumped as he stepped back. No point in taking his frustration out on somebody else. "We're kind of having a problem."

"She doesn't take him seriously," Aidan offered.

Hamilton nodded. "Ah."

"You've been there, I guess?" Tyler asked.

"No, not really."

"Love'll get you, too," Tyler warned. "Just wait."

Hamilton looked a bit wistful. "It hasn't so far."

"Gentlemen…" Aidan extended his hand toward the back door. "I think this discussion calls for more whiskey and the privacy of the library."

"Sloan told me to wait here," Tyler said. "She wants to introduce me to the crowd."

"Don't worry," Aidan said. "She'll know where to—" He stopped as his attention caught on something in the direction of the house.

Sloan was exiting the back door. And just behind her, in a red sundress that glowed beneath the spotlights, was Andrea.

Tyler's heart slammed into his chest.

"That's my Sloan," Aidan murmured.

As the women headed straight toward them, Tyler had a moment to regret the setting. Much as he appreciated the party, the things he needed to say were best told without an audience.

Once she reached the group, Sloan planted her hand on her shapely hip, fanning her face with the other. "All these beautiful men in one place. I think I need something cold to drink." Looping one arm each around Aidan and Carr, she led them off.

Andrea's amused gaze followed them for a second, then she focused on Tyler. His breath caught at the brightness in her pale green eyes. "Can we talk somewhere private?"

His pulse picked up speed and hope surged through his body. He reached for her hand, pulling her closer. "The gazebo is a little crowded right now."

Smiling, she said, "I know a place that isn't."

She led him around a group of palm trees to a side door, then up the back stairs from the kitchen, the same ones they'd taken the night of the costume ball.

When he recognized where they were headed, he knew everything was going to be okay. Perfect, even.

As soon as he closed the door of the blue bedroom behind them, she threw her arms around his neck and kissed him. Her mouth was hungry, persuasive, needy, and he reveled in every touch and breath. There'd been moments in the last few days that he wondered if he'd ever touch her again.

Those fears fell away, replaced by a love so strong and sure he wondered how his heart had ever beat on its own before.

She leaned back and met his gaze. "I've been an idiot."

"I've been an idiot," he returned.

They shared another smile before he led her to the bed, pulling her down to sit beside him. "Ladies first," he invited.

She kept a hold on his hand and her gaze focused intently on his. "I'm sorry about Saturday, the things I said, the way I said them. I'd been unfairly blaming you for the past. I felt like you forced me to protect my heart after you broke it."

"I'm sor—"

She laid her finger over his lips. "You did nothing wrong." She drew her hand down his chest, resting it at his waist. "Actually, I'm glad we didn't get together then. I didn't really love you. I loved a fantasy. I used the facts I knew about you—your sisters' names, what you ate for lunch, your football stats—and drew up the perfect man in my mind. I didn't really know *you*.

"I didn't know about your loyalty to your family and your unit, or the pressure you felt to live up to being a hero." She slid her hand across his thigh. "I didn't know how the people you work with both respect and genuinely like you or about the scar on your knee. Or how considerate you are, remembering Finn likes his coffee sweet. I didn't know you'd never care about who I was, but who I am." Tears in her eyes, she pressed her lips gently to his. "Now I know you. And I know you belong with me, because no one will ever love you more than I do."

Incredibly moved, he crushed her against his chest. "You're all I'll ever need, the only woman I'll ever love. And Saturday was my fault, too. I compared loving you to liking the same TV shows. I didn't exactly come up with a romantic idea." Sliding his hand into his pants pocket, he let go of her long enough to drop to one knee in front of her. "I'm hoping to do better this time."

Her gaze darted from him to the box he held out. Her eyes widened. "You really are serious."

"Very," he said as he flipped open the box and pulled out the diamond solitaire. "Marry me."

"Oh, wow. I…"

"You need some time to think about it?"

"No. No way." She held out her left hand. "I mean, no, I don't need to think about it but, yes about—"

He kissed her and slid the ring on her finger at the same time.

"It's beautiful," she whispered against his cheek, then paused, her sharp brain obviously aligning the details. "And it fits."

"Finn helped pick it out."

"Finn? How long have you had this?"

"Since Saturday afternoon." He pressed her onto the mattress. "I arrested Roger, then went straight to the jeweler."

She cupped his jaw. "You were that sure of me?"

"No. But I wasn't giving up until I had you."

She smiled. "Mission accomplished."

He began unbuttoning her dress. "My most important case." He pressed his lips to the pulse beating rapidly at the base of her throat. "I've missed you."

She wrapped her arms and legs around him. "I got ready thinking of you, and the moment you might undress me later."

Trailing his lips down her chest, he inhaled her familiar citrus scent. "I'm always happy to serve."

That was when he knew she meant she'd literally dressed for him.

The bra was a screaming red that matched her sundress, the panties blue with white stars. If his constituents could see her campaign strategy, he would have won unanimously.

However, he wasn't sharing.

She belonged to him, forever. Every inch of her smooth skin and curvy body would be explored and cherished. Every smart comment from her mouth would draw a smile from his own. Every moment of fidelity and support would be returned a hundredfold.

When their bodies were one, he knew their hearts were as well, drawing a whole new element of intimacy he hadn't expected. Their hands linked, their fingers intertwined as he rocked against her hips, and the moment her neck arched and she closed her eyes while her climax broke and his followed, he knew completeness for the first time in his life.

Wherever he'd gone, whatever had come before, had led him here, to her, to this woman who'd love him with her whole heart, just as he'd devote himself to her.

He tried to catch his breath as he rolled onto his back beside her. "Oh, wow is exactly right."

She wrapped her right hand around his arm, holding her left above them, studying the ring, which glinted in the glare of the spotlight coming through the window. "It's perfect," she said in a dreamy voice he'd rarely heard from his practical math whiz. "I especially like the sterling silver setting."

Weakly turning his head, he kissed her shoulder. "I thought you might appreciate the significance."

"I do." She sighed. "I guess we should go back to the party."

That innate responsibility was *his* girl.

He thought of Aidan, the way he knew Sloan's determination would bring Andrea as she'd promised. He was starting to understand the woman he'd spend his life with in the same way.

He shifted onto his side, then he drew the tip of his finger down the center of her bare body. "We didn't before."

"But this party's in your honor."

"Good point. What about London?"

Startled, she looked at him. "I'm supposed to leave the day after tomorrow."

"Do you want to go?"

"No."

"You were just running from me."

"I did have a job."

"Uh-huh."

She waved that away with a flip of her hand. "I'll canc—" She stopped, a smile breaking across her beautiful face. "Come with me."

"What?"

Naked, she leaped to her feet. She grabbed her clothes from the floor and started putting them on. "You've got a passport, don't you?"

"Sure, but—"

"You don't take office until January, right?"

"Well, yeah."

Impulsive and practical. Could a woman be both? His certainly was.

The more he considered the idea—three weeks in London with Andrea—the more he knew it was right. After all the tension and anxious days, they could enjoy simply being together. "I'm due for a vacation after solving the biggest crime spree on the island in a decade."

"Exactly."

They dressed in a frenzied haste, then darted out of the room and down the hall. He was already thinking of the people he needed to call about his spontaneous trip when he remembered. "Sloan."

"She can't come," Andrea said as they moved down the stairs.

"No, I mean I promised to let her introduce me onstage."

Andrea stopped. "Now?"

"Tonight anyway."

Andrea took his hand and led him out the side door. "I guess these are the things I have to expect if I'm going to be the wife of a public figure."

He jerked her against him for a quick kiss. "Have I told you how much I love you?"

She stroked his face. "A couple of times, but let's keep it up. My fantasy engagement to you was pretty spectacular. The real one has a lot to live up to."

When they reached Sloan, she was toe-tapping impatiently by the stage. "Where have you two been? I'm supposed to introduce Tyler to—" She stopped, her gaze roving their faces, which were probably still flushed with pleasure and happiness. "Oh." She smiled widely. "I guess you worked out your issues."

Andrea simply held out her left hand. "We did. Thanks."

The two women embraced briefly before somebody shoved a microphone in Sloan's face. "The band's getting impatient."

"Yeah, yeah," she said, grabbing the microphone. "Details tomorrow," she said to Andrea

Next, Sloan was onstage, thanking everyone for coming and for their election day support. She introduced the mayor, then Sheriff Caldwell, her voice breaking a bit when she hugged him and expressed the island's gratitude for his many years of service.

"So, now," she said dramatically, "please welcome the man who will serve and protect our island for many years to come, Sheriff Tyler Landry."

Tyler took the stage to a round of applause and cheers. He shook hands with everyone near the podium and waved at the familiar people in the crowd—his family, Sister Mary Katherine, Aqua, Dwayne and Misty. He'd make sure his life was spent keeping theirs safe, understanding how precious the gift of love and contentment could be.

When the noise died down, he moved toward Sloan to take the microphone, mentally going through the list of people who'd helped him get here, when Sloan pointed toward Andrea. "And please welcome the future Mrs. Landry."

Tyler's gaze darted to Andrea, expecting her reluctance to announce their engagement so publicly and suddenly, but she was already racing up the stairs to join him.

To stand by his side always.

*Rancher Ramsey Westmoreland's temporary cook
is way too attractive for his liking.
Little does he know Chloe Burton came to
his ranch with another agenda entirely....*

That man across the street had to be, without a doubt, the most handsome man she'd ever seen.

Chloe Burton's pulse beat rhythmically as he stopped to talk to another man in front of a feed store. He was tall, dark and every inch of sexy—from his Stetson to the well-worn leather boots on his feet. And from the way his jeans and Western shirt fit his broad muscular shoulders, it was quite obvious he had everything it took to separate the men from the boys. The combination was enough to corrupt any woman's mind and had her weakening even from a distance. Her body felt flushed. It was hot. Unsettled.

Over the past year the only male who had gotten her time and attention had been the e-mail. That was simply pathetic, especially since now she was practically drooling simply at the sight of a man. Even his stance—both hands in his jeans pockets, legs braced apart, was a pose she would carry to her dreams.

And he was smiling, evidently enjoying the conversation being exchanged. He had dimples, incredibly sexy dimples in not one but both cheeks.

"What are you staring at, Clo?"

Chloe nearly jumped. She'd forgotten she had a lunch date. She glanced over the table at her best friend from college, Lucia Conyers.

"Take a look at that man across the street in the blue shirt, Lucia. Will he not be perfect for Denver's first issue of *Simply Irresistible* or what?" Chloe asked with so much excitement she almost couldn't stand it.

She was the owner of *Simply Irresistible*, a magazine for today's up-and-coming woman. Their once-a-year Irresistible Man cover, which highlighted a man the magazine felt deserved the honor, had increased sales enough for Chloe to open a Denver office.

When Lucia didn't say anything but kept staring, Chloe's smile widened. "Well?"

Lucia glanced across the booth at her. "Since you asked, I'll tell you what I see. One of the Westmorelands—Ramsey Westmoreland. And yes, he'd be perfect for the cover, but he won't do it."

Chloe raised a brow. "He'd get paid for his services, of course."

Lucia laughed and shook her head. "Getting paid won't be the issue, Clo—Ramsey is one of the wealthiest sheep ranchers in this part of Colorado. But everyone knows what a private person he is. Trust me—he won't do it."

Chloe couldn't help but smile. The man was the epitome of what she was looking for in a magazine cover and she was determined that whatever it took, he would be it.

"Umm, I don't like that look on your face, Chloe. I've seen it before and know exactly what it means."

She watched as Ramsey Westmoreland entered the store with a swagger that made her almost breathless. She *would* be seeing him again.

* * * * *

Look for Silhouette Desire's
HOT WESTMORELAND NIGHTS by Brenda Jackson,
available March 9 wherever books are sold.

HARLEQUIN *Presents*

Two families torn apart by secrets and desire
are about to be reunited in

Hot Bed of Scandal

a sexy new duet by

Kelly Hunter

EXPOSED: MISBEHAVING WITH THE MAGNATE

#2905 Available March 2010

Gabriella Alexander returns to the French vineyard she
was banished from after being caught in flagrante with the
owner's son Lucien Duvalier—only to finish what they started!

REVEALED: A PRINCE AND A PREGNANCY

#2913 Available April 2010

Simone Duvalier wants Rafael Alexander and always has, but
they both get more than they bargained for when a night of
passion and a royal revelation rock their world!

REQUEST YOUR FREE BOOKS!

2 FREE NOVELS PLUS 2 FREE GIFTS!

HARLEQUIN®

Blaze

Red-hot reads!

HB10

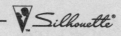

SPECIAL EDITION

FROM *USA TODAY* BESTSELLING AUTHOR

CHRISTINE RIMMER

A BRIDE FOR JERICHO BRAVO

Marnie Jones had long ago buried her wild-child
impulses and opted to be "safe," romantically
speaking. But one look at born rebel Jericho Bravo
and she began to wonder if her thrill-seeking side
was about to be revived. Because if ever there was
a man worth taking a chance on, there he was,
right within her grasp....

*Available in March
wherever books are sold.*

HARLEQUIN® *Blaze*

COMING NEXT MONTH

Available February 23, 2010

#525 BLAZING BEDTIME STORIES, VOLUME IV
Bedtime Stories
Kimberly Raye and Samantha Hunter

#526 TOO HOT TO HANDLE
Forbidden Fantasies
Nancy Warren

#527 HIS LITTLE BLACK BOOK
Encounters
Heather MacAllister

#528 LONE STAR LOVER
Stolen from Time
Debbi Rawlins

#529 POSSESSING MORGAN
Bonnie Edwards

#530 KNOWING THE SCORE
Marie Donovan

www.eHarlequin.com